IRON EYES IS DEAD

Desert Springs was an oasis that drew the dregs of Texas down into its profitable boundaries. Among the many ruthless characters, there was none so fearsome as the infamous bounty hunter, Iron Eyes. He had trailed a dangerous outlaw right into the remote settlement. But Iron Eyes was wounded: shot up with arrow and bullet after battling with a band of Apaches. As the doctor fought to save him, was the call true that Iron Eyes was dead?

RORY BLACK

IRON EYES
IS DEAD

Complete and Unabridged

LINFORD
Leicester

First published in Great Britain in 2010 by
Robert Hale Limited
London

First Linford Edition
published 2012
by arrangement with
Robert Hale Limited
London

British Library CIP Data

Black, Rory.
    Iron Eyes is dead.- -(Linford western library)
    1. Bounty hunters- -Texas- -Fiction.
    2. Western stories. 3. Large type books.
    I. Title II. Series
    823.9'2–dc23

    ISBN 978–1–4448–1020–2

Published by
F. A. Thorpe (Publishing)
Anstey, Leicestershire

Set by Words & Graphics Ltd.
Anstey, Leicestershire
Printed and bound in Great Britain by
T. J. International Ltd., Padstow, Cornwall

This book is printed on acid-free paper

*Dedicated to the actor,
western star and stunt rider
Dick Jones*

Prologue

The sweltering heat haze twisted the burning air before the horseman's sand-grazed eyes. Images in a sickening soup mocked him. It was like a tormenting rattlesnake drawing him towards its lethal fangs. Yet the tall palomino stallion remained sturdy as it obeyed the sharp spurs of its new master. Even in this unforgiving climate the powerful animal continued to forge on as the sun grew increasingly hot the higher it rose above the vast expanse of blistering sand. But it was not the sun nor the heat which filled the mind of the rider. It was the deep hoof-tracks of his prey in the white-hot sand that lured the emaciated horseman ever onward in his quest to administer his own form of justice once and for all. They were like a magnet to the deep-set bullet-coloured eyes of the deadly rider.

1

A lure that he was helpless to ignore.

The sun was now directly overhead and both man and beast were beginning to flag. This was a place where shadows disappeared at the very time when they were most needed. The rider allowed the stallion to stop and lower its head. Rolling dunes surrounded them. Dunes which appeared to move as the hot air played tricks with his bleeding eyes. He raised a hand and vainly rubbed at the cruel grains of sand which filled them. It made no difference. A million crazed hornets could not have stung more. He stared at the blood on his fingertips and spat to his side, then pulled a cigar from his deep jacket pocket. He placed it between his teeth and ran a match across the saddle horn. It ignited. He cupped its flame and sucked in the strong smoke.

It felt good.

He concentrated. All that lay ahead was a vast expanse of more sand with the trail of his human prey imprinted upon its dry surface. Smoke drifted from between his small sharp teeth as they gripped the cigar firmly.

He smiled.

It was a knowing smile. A cruel smile. He knew that there would be no escape this time for the outlaw who had already managed to outwit him once.

The bounty hunter knew that however hard Joe Brewster rode the powerful beast beneath his saddle he would eventually catch up to him. However cunning the outlaw might have been up until now, Brewster was doomed to follow the same fate that the bounty hunter had already dished out to the outlaw's two brothers.

Death was the only certainty.

Death was inevitable once Iron Eyes had the scent of his prey in his flared nostrils. And he had inhaled that aroma a long way back on the trail to this unholy place. The thin figure tapped the ash from his cigar and then returned it to his mouth and sucked hard. As acrid smoke drifted all around his face he saw something through the hot pitiless air.

Something which he knew might slow his progress or even bring it to an abrupt halt.

The bony hands released their grip on the reins and wrapped the long leathers around the saddle horn. He raised his arms and then forced his fingers through his matted mane of long black hair until every scar upon his hideous face was visible. Every fight and battle he had endured over the years could be seen in the twisted flesh which had once been a face like so many other faces.

The fearless rider narrowed his eyes and gave out a long sigh. Then he leaned back to his saddlebags and plucked a bottle of whiskey from one of the satchels. He pulled its cork, raised the bottle to his lips and sucked in the fiery liquor. With every swallow his unblinking eyes watched the half-dozen Apaches who sat astride their ponies. Tellingly, they stared right back at him.

Any other man might have gone unnoticed or even ignored by the hunting party of near-naked braves, but not Iron Eyes. It was as though every native of this vast land had heard of him in the myths which spilled from the mouths of elders around their camp-fires. The trouble was, they believed every word of the legend, which grew with each telling.

It was said that Iron Eyes hated Indians.

So Indians hated Iron Eyes.

The truth was far simpler. Since the strange hunter of men had first emerged from the dense forests far to the north-west his appearance had never allowed anyone truely to claim him as one of their own.

He was a misfit.

For Iron Eyes did not fully resemble either white or red man, yet he had similarities to both.

He was tall and thin, like many a white man, yet with naturally tanned skin and long black hair and a face which refused to grow any facial hair, like an Indian.

He was both feared and rejected by them all.

To the Indians and the white men alike, he was vermin. Men killed vermin, or at least tried to kill them. It was what men did.

Iron Eyes continued to stare with deadly intent at the Apaches who were blocking his advance. It was a situation he had experienced many times before with various tribes. Each time it had ended in bloodshed. Each time he had managed to survive and carry on.

Still watching them with narrowed eyes, he slowly lowered the bottle and rubbed his mouth along the sleeve of his tattered trail jacket. He returned the cork and pushed it down into the bottle's neck.

They were young bucks.

Probably no more than half his age but they recognized the legendary figure before them from the stories they had been raised with.

To most tribes Iron Eyes was a ghost. An evil spirit who could never be killed because he was already dead. Yet they always wanted to test the theory. For the warrior who did manage to kill this fearsome apparition would go down in Indian mythology.

The bony left hand of the bounty hunter pushed the bottle back into the satchel behind his cantle. The sound of it touching the other whiskey bottles rang out across the silent landscape.

One of the Apaches raised a rifle and started to yell out across the fifty or so yards' distance between them. Then the five others joined in the ranting. Although the bounty hunter did not understand one word of the cursing which grew ever louder he knew what it meant.

What it always meant.

It was a challenge.

A challenge from hot-blooded young braves to battle to the death with a mythical being. A creature more than a man in their collective mind. A monster. Iron Eyes was someone whom they knew had never been defeated and yet they had to face and fight him.

There was no other way.

Only cowards sought one.

Angrily, Iron Eyes took a deep breath and tossed his cigar away. He gathered up his reins in his left hand and then curled his long bony fingers around one of his two Navy Colts, which poked out from his pants belt. As the wailing and taunting grew deafening, his thumb clawed back on the gun's hammer until it fully locked.

Iron Eyes slid the weapon from his belt and rested it across the saddle horn in readiness. He lowered his gruesome head and angrily glared at them. Blood traced from both eyes and ran down the scarred features.

'Damn it all!' he cursed with a shake of his head. 'I hate killing Apaches! There ain't no profit in it! No profit at all!'

The stallion beneath him snorted as the horsemen turned their mounts and started towards him.

Iron Eyes raised the gun and then gave out an even more chilling cry. He thrust his spurs back and the palomino charged toward the six braves.

The air soon filled with gunsmoke.

Half the young Apaches had rifles, the other half carried three small bows with deadly flint-tipped arrowheads. Yet within five paces of the huge palomino horse, two of the braves had been punched from the backs of their ponies by the sheer impact of the Navy Colt's lead. The young warriors whipped their mounts with rawhide reins and raced down the dune at the rider who was almost upon them.

Rifles blasted.

Iron Eyes felt the tails of his long trail coat being lifted by the vicious bullets and yet he kept charging. His gun kept spewing out its own retribution.

Then one of the Apaches let an arrow fly from his bow. It did not miss its target. Iron Eyes reeled as the arrow went straight through his thin frame just below his left collarbone. The bounty hunter's horse tore between the four Indians and then was hauled to an abrupt stop. Ignoring his own pain, Iron Eyes dragged the stallion around. The Apaches did exactly the same. They were facing one another again. Blood flowed from the shaft of the arrow in his chest but Iron Eyes refused to quit. He hauled his other gun from his belt and cocked its hammer.

Two more rifle shots blasted from the barrels of their weapons. He felt one tear into his right leg as the other passed over his head.

Iron Eyes steadied his wide-eyed mount and returned fire.

He watched as both riflemen went flying backwards off the backs of their ponies. Even before they had crashed into the sand he had spurred his horse into action again.

The wounded bounty hunter galloped back towards the two remaining Apaches. With every stride of the stallion's long legs, Iron Eyes fired his guns until their smoking chambers were empty.

Iron Eyes dragged rein and stopped his horse.

The sand was crimson.

There was no satisfaction to Iron Eyes in the sight of six dead Apache braves. It had been yet another pointless battle.

As the gunsmoke drifted away, Iron Eyes stared at his bleeding leg and then saw the feathered flight of the arrow a few inches from his face. He went to pull it and then realized that it had gone right through his thin frame. He realized that there was no way he could remove this arrow without killing himself in the process.

'Damn it all!' He cursed again before dropping his guns into his deep coat pocket. 'I bin well and truly skewered this time. I gotta get me some doctoring damn fast!' He swung the horse around and spurred.

The stallion obeyed.

1

The sound of gunfire swept like a tidal wave across the arid landscape. At first it resembled thunderclaps to the ears of the solitary horseman. Then he realized exactly what it had been which had spooked not only his mount but himself. The outlaw pulled back on his reins as the noise of the brief but deadly gun battle resounded around the dry desert air. Joe Brewster stood in his stirrups and looked back with narrowed eyes. Back to where he knew the shots had come from. Every sinew in his aching frame knew who it was back amid the mountains of dunes, unleashing lead. It could only be one person. One man who doggedly refused to quit the chase.

Iron Eyes.

For the first time since he had fled Mexico Brewster realized that the infamous Iron Eyes was still hunting him. Hunting him like most men hunt down game or vermin. The trouble was Brewster knew that he was still the game. The hunted.

A rage burned inside him as he recalled how Iron Eyes had killed both his brothers with no hint of emotion. Wanted dead or alive meant only one thing to Iron Eyes.

It meant dead.

'How can he still be alive?' Brewster snarled nervously. 'I left that fool back in the middle of a Mexican war! Can't anything kill that bastard?'

The rider sat back down on his saddle and brooded. He had known that there were some cold-hearted hunters of men who refused to quit once their dander was up. Iron Eyes was that breed. His kind never turned their backs on a bounty. They kept on coming. Like the Grim Reaper, nothing could sway them from their chosen path or victim.

Brewster gathered his reins up and

then stared at the mountainous dune before him. It appeared to be the biggest one of them all. He lifted his canteen and gave it a shake. Like all the others which hung from his saddle horn, it was as dry as the sand beneath his horse's hoofs. He rubbed his gloved hand across his mouth and felt his lips crack and begin to bleed.

The sight of black wide-winged vultures floating on high thermals chilled the outlaw. They were circling. They had sensed the recent kill. They would feast on the carcass whether it be human or beast regardless, before sundown.

It was now more than two days since he had used up the last of his water and he hurt bad. Thirst was a mighty hard thing to handle. His left hand pulled out a well-worn map from his vest pocket. He shook its fragile paper until it unfolded before him. Brewster stared at the crude map his brother Clem had drawn for them. Clearly marked was a town amid wooded terrain at the edge of the desert. That was where they were meant to go and catch a stagecoach north to Waco. He patted the canvas bags of coins and paper money which he no longer had to share with his siblings.

But would he ever reach that town which Clem had insisted was there above the desert? Brewster doubted it. He was a rich man but feared that soon he would be a rich dead man.

He had followed the stars through the desert just as Clem had taught him. Stayed exactly on course, yet all he could see was that damn big expanse of sand. He knew that he had not wavered off the route set down on the map. Now he wondered whether there was really a town out here at all? Had Clem got mixed up? Could there be a town out here in the middle of this hell?

The outlaw gritted his teeth and screwed up the map into a tight ball. He tossed it away and growled. He was going to die out here because of a dumb map made by his even dumber brother.

That was the truth of it.

Brewster glanced upward for a few seconds and then realized that if the souls of his brothers were anywhere it was not up there. He lifted himself up and balanced in his stirrups to take the weight off his mount's back. He lashed the shoulders of his lathered-up horse until it began to react. The horse obeyed its master's desperate exhortations and the sound of the leathers as they cracked against the dry air to either side. The animal climbed the steep dune of sand slowly but never once lost its footing.

When both horse and rider reached the flat top of the slope of soft, shifting sand he caught sight of the very thing he had begun to believe did not exist. Then a smile crossed his features as his tired eyes focused on the town a quarter of a mile ahead of him. Its countless windows caught the rays of the sun and glinted like precious jewels.

Brewster steadied the animal beneath him. The scent of fresh water filled both their nostrils.

'So that's Desert Springs!' The outlaw sighed thankfully. 'Clem was right all the time!'

Desert Springs stood in the heart of an oasis. The land was filled with grass and trees. So many trees that he was unable to count them all.

Joe Brewster ran a glove along the neck of his horse and gave a last glance backward to where he knew the shooting had come from. It was so hot back there that the air made it impossible for him to see anything clearly. Hell on earth, he thought. Only Iron Eyes would willingly ride into terrain such as that in pursuit of his prey. If any man was more suited to the bowels of Hell it was the deadly bounty hunter. Iron Eyes had probably not even broken sweat yet, he speculated.

Then another thought filled the outlaw's mind. He wondered whom Iron Eyes had been fighting back there. If it actually was Iron Eyes, that is. Brewster had not seen another living soul in that arid lifeless terrain. Then

18

another thought amused him. What if Iron Eyes was dead? Could one of those shots which had echoed around the vast desert have actually claimed the monstrous creature who kept on following him?

It was a mouth-watering thought.

'C'mon, boy!' The outlaw urged the animal beneath him to continue on towards the town. The scent of the fresh water in both their flared nostrils drew them on.

It was a sweet smell.

It was the aroma of life in an otherwise land of death.

* * *

The bounty hunter refused to listen to or heed the screams from his wounded body. Soaked in his own blood Iron Eyes defiantly pressed on. He swayed in his saddle like a man close to meeting his Maker but Iron Eyes refused to fall. He would continue to pursue the outlaw who, he knew, must now be close. His eagle-like eyes burned as they stared at the marks left in Brewster's wake. The hoof tracks left by the outlaw's mount were clearer now. Iron Eyes stopped the stallion and stared down at them. Even a brain starved of blood noticed the difference from a few miles back. The sand must be getting damper somehow, his fevered mind mused. Hoof-tracks in dry sand were undefined but now he could actually make out the shape of the horse's shoes.

It confused him for a few seconds until his attention was drawn to his own bleeding leg again. The bullet had gone clean through and was embedded in his saddle but that made no difference to the amount of blood he had already lost and was still losing.

He could see the blood pumping from the bullet hole in his thigh. His pants leg was soaked and his boot felt as though it was filled with his precious gore.

Iron Eyes pushed the long lifeless strands of hair from his face, then turned. He reached for the bottle in his saddle-bag and pulled it clear. His teeth drew the cork free and this time he spat it away. He carefully poured whiskey into the hole and gritted his teeth as he felt the fiery liquid make its way right through his leg until it found the bullet's exit wound. A weaker man might have been unable to stop himself from screaming out in agony, but that was not his way. All pain had to be denied, for to admit its fury was to give it power. Iron Eyes gasped and then raised the bottle to his lips. He drank most of what remained and then when there was barely an inch of the amber liquor left in the clear glass vessel he tilted the neck and poured the remnants over the arrow which still protruded from his shoulder both front and back.

Again he fought the pain and refused to scream out. After what felt like an eternity the burning ceased and he felt his heart slow. Sweat now dripped like rain from his bony scarred face but Iron

Eyes did not notice. He tossed the empty bottle away and sighed heavily.

The leg was still pumping blood. Instinctively his bony hands drew his Bowie knife from its hiding-place in the neck of his boot. He used its sharp blade to cut a length of his reins free, then returned the cruel weapon back into his boot. He looped the leather strip around his thin leg and tied a firm knot in it.

The blood did not stop pumping but it slowed a little. His eyes looked up.

There was a scent on the air.

A scent he knew.

It was the scent of his prey. Brewster's sweat lingered on the warm air as it drifted over the arid land. Iron Eyes inhaled deeper and then caught the aroma of another familiar fragrance.

Water.

There was water close. A lot of water. His eyes looked at the head of the stallion who also sniffed at the air. It too had caught the scent.

Iron Eyes spurred once more.

2

The town of Desert Springs was well named. It stood at the very northernmost tip of one of the most arid terrains in all of Texas. Yet unlike the desert around it, this was a lush oasis that continued on for another fifty miles. Few settlements could better it for sweet grazing grassland or its plentiful supply of clear spring water which had never ceased bubbling up from subterranean caverns to fill countless wells. It was a quiet place, which had only occasionally erupted into violence during its short but fruitful existence.

At first a Spanish mission had been established to tame the restless natives but then God gave way to free-thinking men and the town quickly grew around the once dominant whitewashed building. The adobe structure still survived in the very centre of the sprawling town but now it served no purpose except to remind those old enough to remember of times long since gone.

Now Desert Springs boasted more than a hundred buildings which covered twenty acres around the natural spring. The main street covered a quarter of a mile with a dozen side streets branching off in every direction. Richer folks lived away from the vibrant heart of the town in homes only wealth could have constructed. Yet the majority of those who dwelled within the lush oasis chose to remain in the busy centre of the town. Apart from its location, Desert Springs appeared on the surface to be exactly like a hundred others. Yet it was different in many ways.

Many subtle ways.

Isolation had been a blessing and also a curse to the residents. For years the people had only themselves to encounter on a daily basis. Everyone knew his neighbour and trouble tended to be swiftly dealt with. Then the outside world discovered the remote place, which seemed to have been blessed with more than its share of bounties. The Overland Stage Company had established a regular route to and from Desert Springs and with the invasion of so many outsiders, trouble had started to grow.

Grow like a cancer.

The marshal's office stood in the very middle of the main street. Flanked by a saloon on one side and a hotel on the other it was well placed to handle any trouble which raised its ugly head. And lately trouble had been rife.

For the first time in the history of the small settlement it had required the services of a lawman. A damn good lawman. And they had found one.

Laredo-born Marshal Monte Bale had enjoyed his thirteen months in office. Having a deputy made his job far easier than it had been in some of the poorer towns he had frequented during his thirty-seven years of life. A seasoned man who had learned his gun skills long ago as a hired gunfighter, Bale had settled in the quiet town when the wealthy elders of Desert Springs had sought him out to handle their increasingly hostile streets. A marshal who had earned the star he proudly wore on his shirt on the deadly streets of El Paso, Bale had no illusions that this apparent Eden was in fact as dangerous as any he had ever guarded.

The tall, broad-shouldered man leaned against the doorframe of his office and rested a hand on his holstered gun grip. He studied the long street with knowing eyes. He had reached a stage where he actually thought that he could smell trouble brewing long before it ignited into bloody confrontation. People in Desert Springs always acknowledged the lawman with smiles, nods or the simple touch of a hat brim. They all knew that this was a man who could and would risk everything for any one of them should the need arise. Only the strangers who continued to flood into the oasis on the edge of the burning desert did not acknowledge either the man or his authority.

They seemed actually to want trouble. The previous month had already seen three men gunned down for reasons best known to themselves. None of the victims had been local folks. Each had died with far more money in their billfolds than seemed logical and the marshal was curious about that.

A new gambling-hall had been constructed on the end of Main Street by outsiders with deep pockets and an endless supply of hard cash. So far its doors had not opened for business but already the well-dressed owner named Texas Jack Kelly had gathered a dozen gunslingers around him.

The seasoned lawman knew that that was something he had to keep an eye on. It was a tinderbox amid so many naked flames. Any one of which could explode and destroy a small town like this one. Money could buy most things with ease but it could not tempt Monte Bale. He was a man who was satisfied with his monthly pay-check. There was an old saying that you could not con an honest man. You could not bribe or buy him either.

Bale was a man who smiled.

Smiled a lot.

He knew that a smile could unnerve a lot of folks because it showed that he was fearless. After thirteen months Bale knew most local people in Desert Springs by name and that counted for a lot to the people of this town. For it meant that they actually mattered to someone. Someone who wore a star and smile.

But each day the stagecoach seemed to bring in more and more strangers. Drifters with more weaponry than seemed necessary also arrived on horseback, either alone or in pairs. These were faces Bale did not know and a lack of wanted posters only added to his concern.

Marshal Bale was one of the rare breed of men who would actually defend each and every one of them, though. He showed no favour to any of them as long as they behaved themselves. The tall man reached around the door, plucked his hat from its wall hook, then beat it against his right pants leg.

Then, after running his fingers through his black hair, he placed it on his head. His eyes screwed up in anticipation of the glaring sunlight of the street.

'You coming, Joshua?' Bale asked over his shoulder to the thin deputy who was trying to sweep out the cells behind him, beyond the pair of desks.

Joshua Peck was a fast-talking twenty-two-year-old who had been born just 200 yards from the wooden building. A deputy for almost as long as Bale had been a marshal, he looked up when he heard his name being uttered. His eyes brightened as he tossed the broom aside and hurried to the marshal's side.

'Where we going, Monte?'

'Reckon it's about time we had us a bite to eat.' Bale sighed and stepped out into the sunshine.

'Is it breakfast already?' Joshua rubbed his hands together. 'I sure am mighty hungry!'

'It's nearly noon.' Bale closed the door behind them, stepped down into the sandy street and started across towards the café. The younger man hurried beside him. 'We already had breakfast three hours back.'

'I still got room for another one, Marshal.'

The lawman looked at the man beside him and tutted. 'Ain't you feeling a tad naked, Joshua?'

The question caused the deputy to blush. 'I'm wearing my britches, Monte. Why would I be feeling — '

'You forgot your gun again,' Bale corrected. 'How many times have I gotta tell you to always remember to wear your gun, boy? A man can get into trouble as fast a rattler can bite. Always keep your gun strapped around your middle and if trouble happens, you'll be ready.'

'But nothing ever happens around here, Marshal.'

They both reached the opposite boardwalk. Bale paused, turned to his deputy and pointed back at their office.

'Go and get your gun and belt, boy.'

Joshua sniffed at the air. The scent of fresh-brewed coffee and frying steaks filled his nostrils. 'Can't I go get it after we've had our grub?'

Bale lowered his head. His eyes stared straight into Joshua's. He did not speak. He smiled.

'OK! OK! I'll go get my gun and belt!' The deputy shrugged, turned and ran back towards the office.

'Steak?' Bale called out.

'And biscuits and gravy!'

The marshal stepped up on to the boardwalk and rested his hand upon the worn doorknob. As he turned it he caught the reflection of a rider in the café window. The tall lawman released his grip and turned back to face the street. His eyes narrowed as they focused on the horseman who had just entered the town from the direction of the desert.

'Now who the hell is that sorrowful-looking *hombre*?' Bale asked himself. He placed the palm of his left hand on a wooden upright and leaned out into the brilliant sunlight.

Joe Brewster rode like a man who had a thirst and a million saddle sores. His exposed skin was burned and blistered from the desert's fury. When the labouring mount reached the hotel the exhausted rider slid down to the ground and rested both hands on the pump beside the trough as his horse drank.

Bale watched as the outlaw pumped water into the trough and placed his open mouth beneath the crystal-clear liquid. Both man and beast drank feverishly.

The deputy ran back to the the marshal's side and managed to buckle his belt just before he reached the tall, curious Bale. He looked in the direction where the marshal's gaze was focused. He scratched his head at the unexpected sight.

'Well glory be! Now I wonder who that poor-looking critter is, Monte?'

Bale ran his fingers along his strong

jaw. 'Whoever he is he came into town from the wrong direction, Joshua.'

The younger man nodded. 'He sure is thirsty. I ain't never seen anyone that thirsty before and no mistake.'

The marshal nodded without taking his eyes away from the outlaw. 'Wouldn't you be mighty thirsty if'n you'd just crossed that desert?'

Joshua looked at the man beside him. 'I've lived here all my life and I ain't never seen anyone make it here from thataway, Monte. You reckon he did cross the desert?'

Bale slowly nodded. 'Look at them. No man or horse could look that bad without crossing a desert, boy.'

'Must have come up from Mexico,' the keen deputy said.

'Yep!'

Then Joshua inhaled the aromatic scent of the cooking food again. He licked his lips. 'I'm powerful hungry, Monte!'

Marshal Bale pushed the door open and followed his deputy into the cool café. As he closed the door behind them his eyes continued to stare through the window across the wide street at the man who had now staggered into the hotel, carrying his hefty bags of plunder.

'That sure is curious.'

'What ya looking at, Monte?' Joshua asked as he sat down at the nearest table.

'Them bags he's hauling, they sure look mighty heavy, Joshua,' Bale answered. 'As if they're full of coin.'

'Maybe he's a bank robber,' the deputy joked as he clutched a knife and fork eagerly in his hands.

Monte Bale turned and looked down at Joshua. His left eyebrow rose as a smile crossed his features. 'Maybe.'

3

It felt like an eternity to the emaciated rider as he guided his magnificent stallion down through the last of the sand dunes towards the scent of the fresh water. Every stride of the tall horse was agony to the defiant blood-soaked horseman. The arrow in his thin shoulder moved with every jolt of the striding palomino causing the bounty hunter to roll like a rag doll. His almost closed eyes could see the blood continuing to trace from the makeshift tourniquet. Yet his injuries did not worry Iron Eyes. He could sense that at long last they were now closing in on the place to which Brewster must have been headed for these past weeks. Somewhere close there had to be a town or even just an outpost where the outlaw knew he would find salvation. Iron Eyes silently vowed that he too would find that place.

The horse approached the last of the giant mounds of sand as its master leaned back and stared through his limp, long, sweat-soaked hair. The hoof-tracks of the outlaw's horse pointed the way. All he had to do was keep following them.

The mind of the rider was now filled with a stew of thoughts that only fever could have assembled. His bony left hand jerked back on his reins and slowed the animal to a walk.

'Easy, horse!' Iron Eyes growled as his wits alerted him to the possible danger of what might lie ahead. Even half-conscious, the wounded rider knew that the outlaw might be lying in wait for him. Brewster had winged him months earlier when he had been cornered. Iron Eyes did not want the outlaw to repeat the action. He forced himself up off his saddle and balanced in his stirrups as the stallion began, slowly to climb the rise of sand. A swift glance at his bleeding leg was dismissed. Iron Eyes drew one of his Navy Colts and cocked its hammer.

The burning sand and a vast expanse of cloudless sky had not stopped him. The Apaches' bullet and the arrow had only slowed his progress. Only death could have ended his pursuit of the outlaw Joe Brewster.

'Dead or alive,' he kept repeating.

After what felt like a lifetime the horse reached the top of the vast dune. Iron Eyes dropped back down on to his saddle and gave out a long weary sigh. The sickening air still played its tricks to his eyes but now the rider either did not notice or did not give a damn. Only when a man was this close to death did he feel truly immortal.

He rubbed his eyes and then saw the town. He could hear the people in its streets going about their rituals. This was no mirage, he told himself. It was there. It was real. Iron Eyes released the hammer of his gun and pushed it back into his belt against his flesh.

Then tentatively he eased his emaciated frame off the horse and rested against the saddle. His thin legs were unsteady but even they still somehow obeyed him. He tightened the leather around his thigh and watched as the blood slowed its flow from the bullet hole. He reached up. His fingers clawed at the cool water bag before dragging it free.

As it hit the sand he produced the Bowie knife and sliced through its leather to expose what remained of the precious water. The stallion stepped back, then lowered its head and began to drink.

'Drink ya fill, boy. You earned it.'

Iron Eyes found a cigar and pushed it into his mouth. He struck a match and sucked in the smoke. It did not help. He coughed and then angrily threw the smouldering weed away.

He reached for the nearest satchel. His fingers found a full bottle and he clutched it to his chest. Iron Eyes was angry with the outlaw who had managed to avoid his bullets for so long. No one had ever been that lucky before. He tugged the cork from the neck of the bottle and spat it away as he slid slowly down to the sand beside the horse's legs. He raised the whiskey bottle and began to drink. The fiery liquid tasted like water. He could not understand it.

Iron Eyes lowered the bottle and looked at the contents inside its clear glass. It was whiskey all right. Again he took a swig and swallowed it. Again it seemed to have no flavour.

He shook his head and then poured the whiskey freely over his wounds. He felt it burn like a forest fire. It was whiskey, he told himself. After a few moments Iron Eyes tried to get back to his feet.

Suddenly, for the first time in his memory, his legs refused to obey. He placed the empty bottle in the sand, reached up to the closest stirrup and clutched it. It would take every ounce of his willpower and evaporating strength to pull himself up but that was what he did. After what felt like a lifetime Iron Eyes was back on his feet, clinging to the saddle.

Somehow Iron Eyes had managed the feat. He clung to the drinking animal's saddle and knew that now he would have to climb back up on top of the tall animal if he were to reach the town that lay below. He screwed up his eyes and looked at the horse beside him. This was no Indian pony, he thought.

This was a pure-bred Mexican horse which was fit for nobility, far taller than all the other animals he had tortured over the years. He felt weak. A mountain could not have offered the bounty hunter a more formidable challenge.

He had to get back in the saddle again, he told himself. But how? To fail was to die. The desert was merciless and took no prisoners. So hot that even sidewinders refused to move across the smooth, fine ocean of sand during the

40

day. He had to get back on top of this tall creature or he would be buzzard bait.

Hell itself could not have been hotter or more dangerous to anything still clutching to life. He tried to raise his good leg but the injured one could not take his weight. He then tried to raise his wounded leg but it would not respond to his cursing.

'Damn it all!' Iron Eyes growled.

Iron Eyes blinked hard and concentrated harder than he had ever done before. If he could not climb up on the horse then he had to make the creature come down low. Low enough for him to virtually crawl on to the saddle. Holding the reins firmly with one hand, he pulled the Winchester out of its scabbard with the other. The severely wounded bounty hunter began to tap the back of the stallion's knees with the long rifle barrel. The animal's legs bent, then it dropped down until it was kneeling. Through the entire action it continued to satisfy its thirst as Iron

Eyes tossed the seldom-used rifle away. With pain carving its way through his every sinew, Iron Eyes climbed on to the saddle and forced his boots into the stirrups. He sat with the reins firmly gripped in his hands and waited for the horse to stand again.

More dead than alive Iron Eyes patiently waited. Each beat of his pounding heart felt as though life was slipping away from him. But he was unafraid. Death held no fear to the man who had dispatched so many to Boot Hill.

Then his bullet-coloured eyes focused again on the trail left by Brewster's horse's hoofs. A cruel smile crossed his face as the stallion rose up from the sand and snorted with satisfaction.

'See that town down there, boy?' Iron Eyes asked the powerful animal beneath him. 'We're headed there to find us a doctor to patch me up and then we'll find and kill that low-down dirty varmint called Joe Brewster.'

The stallion shook its mane of golden

hair as though it understood the rider it carried. It dragged a hoof across the sand as though it were a bull faced by a matador.

Iron Eyes knew that he had to look after the strong creature beneath his saddle. Without it he would never have survived this painful trek. For the first time Iron Eyes realized that he would never find another horse to replace this mighty stallion.

'You sure ain't no Indian pony,' he praised his animal again.

Again the horse snorted.

Defiantly Iron Eyes dismissed the brutal pain which tortured his body's every movement. He raised his long leathers and slapped rein.

The golden stallion began to descend the slope carrying its dishevelled charge. Dust rose up into the blue heavens with every stride of the powerful palomino. Iron Eyes urged the horse on as his eyes focused straight ahead.

He was closing in on his prey.

The stallion raised its noble head and began to increase its pace.

'C'mon, boy! He's so close I can smell his fear,' Iron Eyes said through gritted teeth as he stared at Desert Springs.

The horse thundered on.

4

The foyer of the Desert Hotel had been practically empty, apart from Rufe Carter, the manager, who sat behind his desk as he carefully browsed through his newspaper. It seemed like so many other afternoons to the man with the handlebar moustache and well-oiled hair, until a shadow traced across the foyer and fell upon his paper. Carter looked up and then blinked hard. The sight of the sun-blistered outlaw carrying his hefty bags towards him made the well-dressed man lower the single sheet of typeprint and swallow drily. There had been many strangers in town lately, but none had ever looked quite like Joe Brewster looked. It was clear that the outlaw had taken the most dangerous route to Desert Springs. One which most failed to complete.

Carter raised an arm and loosened

his stiff collar with an ink-stained finger. He then gulped again. Again there was no spittle. At first sight the man who laboured with the swollen bags would not have been made welcome, but as the dusty outlaw approached the desk Carter knew that he had better keep his lip buttoned.

Perhaps it was the pair of holstered guns strapped to the hips of the stranger that had caused Carter to be cautious. It might have been the fact that this man looked as though he had just escaped from the desert which cooled the manager's normally blunt tongue. Men could get ornery when their brains had been boiled out there in the desert.

Perhaps it was the outlaw's eyes that had frozen the soul of the hotel man. These were the eyes of someone who looked as though he knew how to kill and was ready to do so at any moment. Carter rose from his chair and rested the palms of his shaking hands on the desk to either side of the thick, open register. He cleared his throat, forced a smile, then picked up the pen and dipped its nib into the inkwell.

'Hello,' Carter forced himself to say as he offered the primed writing-tool to Brewster. 'Room?'

Joe Brewster exhaled and gave a slow nod. He accepted the pen and scrawled something approximating to his name across the page. He then lowered the pen and rested it beside the inkwell before turning and glancing at the street through the open doorway. Even though he had not seen any sign of the bounty hunter for weeks he still expected the gaunt, dishevelled figure to appear at any moment. Only killing Iron Eyes could stop the fear which haunted the outlaw.

Carter spun the book and studied the name carefully.

'How long do you think you will be with us, Mr Brewbaker?' Carter asked.

'That depends,' Brewster answered as his left hand pulled a golden half-eagle from his vest pocket and placed it down on the open register. 'How long will that buy me a room for?'

'Over a month.' Carter smiled as he scooped up the coin and looked at its perfect golden surface. 'Don't see many fresh-minted half-eagles in these parts.'

'You can keep the change,' Brewster said in a low tone.

'That's most generous.' Carter's eyes lit up. He turned and plucked a key from a dozen others off the rack behind him. He handed the key to the outlaw. 'Here. The best room in the house — and we have many good rooms.'

Brewster accepted the key and stared at it. 'Number Three. Is that facing the street?'

'It certainly is, Mr Brewbaker.' Carter slipped the coin into his pants pocket. 'If you open the window you can stretch your legs on the veranda. We have a wonderful view of the desert from up there!'

'I already seen the desert, mister,' Brewster growled. 'I tasted the desert and I'm carrying a lot of it in every crack in my damn body right now. What I need is a tub of hot soapy water and a tailor to sell me some new duds.'

'I'll have a tub sent up to the room and you'll be soaking before the hour is out.' Carter nodded firmly. 'I can also have a tailor come to your room to take your order.'

'Good!' The outlaw nodded and looked at the ceiling as though he were actually able to see through it. 'Is there a staircase from the street to this veranda of yours?'

'No sir,' Carter replied.

Brewster smiled wide and true. 'Good! I'd hate for anyone to come visiting me from the street. Folks can get themselves killed thataway. Savvy?'

Carter nodded nervously. 'I . . . I imagine so!'

The outlaw looked at the staircase. The carpet was new and still remained free of damage from spurs. He rubbed his unshaven face and then raised an eyebrow at the hotel manager.

'Some folks might be looking for me.'

'Do you wish me to tell them where you are, sir?'

'That also depends. One man who might be looking for me is real ugly. He looks like a tall, thin scarecrow with long black hair. If he comes looking for me you better tell him I'm someplace else.'

Rufe Carter was just about to object when he saw another golden half-eagle being pushed towards him. He smiled and, as fast as a cardsharp could deal from the bottom of a deck, pocketed the money. 'No problem! If an ugly man with long hair asks for you I shall indeed divert his attention.'

'And warn me,' Brewster added firmy. 'You'll have to warn me fast coz that critter will try to kill me. That'll be worth another half-eagle.'

Carter smiled broadly. 'Excellent!'

The outlaw again glanced at the street. 'Another man named Texas Jack Kelly might be looking for me. If he does I'll be much obliged if'n you show him to my room personally.'

'Texas Jack Kelly.' Carter repeated the name. 'I don't think I know the man but if he announces himself I shall escort him to your room immediately.'

'I like you, pardner,' Brewster said. 'What they call you?'

'Rufe. Rufe Carter.'

Brewster nodded and adjusted the bags on his shoulder. The sound of coins mingling with paper filled the hotel foyer as the outlaw aimed his scuffed boots away from the desk. 'If you play my game, Rufe, you'll be a lot richer than you ever dreamed you would be. OK?'

'OK!'

Brewster turned his head and looked at the man carefully. 'I like that suit of yours. Get that tailor to bring me one like that as well as some trail gear.'

Carter ran his finger down his suit. 'That I will!'

'Get the livery stable man to come and take my horse and bed it down.' Brewster pulled a five-dollar bill from his pants pocket and placed it on the edge of the desk. 'That ought to cover it.'

Carter smiled. 'Consider it done. I shall ensure your horse is well taken care of.'

The outlaw headed to the staircase and slowly walked up towards its landing. With each step the sound of coins rang out from one of the hefty bags through the hotel foyer. The manager of the hotel rubbed his chin and then rushed to the open doorway. He snapped his fingers and a small boy ran to him. Carter gave the boy a nickel.

'Go to the livery and tell Bronson to come here, boy.'

The child ran with the shiny coin clutched in his small hand. Carter looked at the horse at the hitching rail. It was in the same state as its owner, he thought. As he made his way across the foyer back to his desk the hotel manager began to think about his new guest more carefully. He had seen bags like the ones Brewster carried before.

Banks used bags exactly like them to

transfer money in.

Carter sat down and picked his newspaper up again, yet he was unable to concentrate on it. All he could think about were the bags as his imagination began to attempt to calculate how much money might be in their canvas-and-leather bellies.

Far too much for a filthy drifter.

His fingers pulled at the desk drawer until it opened a few inches and enabled him to view its contents. The Colt .45 had seldom been used but that made no difference. He closed the drawer again and then stood up. He opened a door behind him.

'You out there, Charlie?' he yelled out. 'Get a tub and take it up to room three and then take up hot water.'

Rufe Carter walked back to his desk and pulled out the gleaming golden coins he had just been given. His fingers began to sweat.

'How many more of these beautiful things have you got in them bags of yours, Mr Brewbaker?' he whispered.

5

Little escaped the attention of the handsome John Wesley Kelly as he stood outside his magnificent gambling house while the last finishing touches were added to its already gleaming façade. The nameboard was being raised by a half-dozen burly workmen whilst he and his small army of gunmen stood watching. As the name of The Texas House was being nailed into position directly above the double-door entrance the gambler looked along the long main thoroughfare towards the hotel.

Like all men of his dubious profession Kelly was always poker-faced. Whatever he was thinking remained a secret to all onlookers. He placed a thumb in a silk vest pocket and kept watching the hotel rather than his own gambling hall.

Although Texas Jack had not been in Desert Springs long he had already made his mark. A mark which was bloody and caused fear amongst the other businessmen whose trade he was intending to take. Kelly regarded the other gambling-houses in exactly the same way that he regarded a game of poker. If he could steal the pot with a pair of deuces by bluffing, he would. If it took the lead of his henchmen to smother the competition, then that was fine with him as well.

As long as he won the pot.

Three men had died since his arrival in Desert Springs with his heavily armed troop of followers. Men who, like himself, were from other parts of Texas but, unlike himself, unable or unwilling to kill to get what they desired.

The three men who now rested on Boot Hill had thought they were partners with the flamboyant Kelly. In fact they had just been a way for him to get the cash he had required to build his glitzy gambling hall and lay the foundations of an empire.

Kelly sucked on a long Havana and savoured its flavoured smoke. His keen eyes had watched the arrival of the weathered Joe Brewster only moments earlier. As with all skilled gamblers there was no sign of what he actually felt about the sight of the outlaw who carried the hefty money-laden bags. He continued to stare long and hard down the street well after Brewster had dismounted and disappeared into the hotel.

His top gun moved away from the boardwalk beneath the hammering men and the rest of the idle gunslingers to his employer's side. Fargo had been with Kelly for nearly two years and in that short time killed more than five men for him. Unlike many hired guns Fargo never questioned his orders to kill. He actually enjoyed ending people's existence as much as Kelly himself enjoyed a long cigar and a winning hand at poker.

Fargo loosened his bandanna and lifted a boot until it rested on the edge of a trough. He too stared down the street to where the dust- and sweat-covered horse stood.

'Fargo,' Kelly acknowledged.

'What you looking at, Texas Jack?'

Kelly allowed smoke to roll around inside his mouth and then blew a line of it towards the ground.

'Did you see the rider who left that gluepot outside the hotel, Fargo?'

Fargo shrugged and rested his hands on his gun grips. 'Nope. I can't say I was watching the street! I was looking at them boys rupturing themselves with the sign!'

Kelly nodded. 'I did. I saw him.'

'Can't be much of a rider if he got a nag like that between his legs, boss.'

'You'd look like that if'n you rode from Mexico through the desert, Fargo,' Kelly said bluntly.

'But I got me more sense than riding through a desert. I still reckon that only a down and out would ride a horse like that anyplace.' Fargo grinned but saw no reaction in the gambler's face.

The gambler turned and surveyed his sign, then eyed the gunslinger beside him. 'That's where you are wrong, Fargo. The man who rode in on that pitiful horse is very much a man. A real dangerous man.'

Fargo lowered his leg back to the ground and leaned forward, resting his knuckles on his holstered gun grips. 'More dangerous than me or the boys?'

'That has yet to be seen.' Kelly gripped the cigar firmly in his teeth and smiled as the workmen clambered down their ladders to the street. He applauded them for their craftsmanship. 'A mighty fine sign and a job well done! You boys sure know how to build a gambling-hall and no mistake!'

'Thank you kindly, Mr Kelly,' the burliest of the sweating men replied.

The gunman ran the palm of his left hand across his sweating neck and moved in front of Texas Jack. Their eyes met. Again there was no hint of emotion of any kind in the eyes of the gambler.

'Who is he, Texas Jack?'

There was a long silence as Kelly produced a wad of bills from his pocket and started to count out six of the crisp fives for the carpenters.

'Who is he?' Fargo repeated the question.

'Joe Brewster Kelly,' answered without blinking. 'Have you heard of him?'

Fargo slowly nodded. 'Sure, I've heard of the Brewster brothers, boss. How come he's alone? I thought them boys were glued together at the hip!'

'That is something I have yet to find out.' Kelly pulled the cigar from his lips and tapped the ash with his index finger; then returned the expensive smoke back to his mouth. 'I was expecting all three of them. You're right, Fargo. Why is Joe on his lonesome? That is a mighty troubling question. Something must have gone wrong.'

'You sent for them Brewsters?' Fargo

looked offended. 'What you go calling for them for? Ain't me and the boys good enough to handle this town for you any more?'

Kelly lowered his head. He glared at the ground. 'You and the men you have recruited are the best there is, Fargo. My business with the Brewster boys has nothing to do with my hiring them. They ain't gunslingers, they're bank robbers.'

'Then why'd you send for them?' Fargo was confused. 'You figuring on robbing the bank in this town?'

'Nope.' Kelly sighed. 'I have a lot of my own money in that bank. Seems a tad pointless.'

Fargo shuffled his boots like a child who had suddenly discovered that he was no longer the favourite. 'Then why'd you send for them? Why send for a pack of lowdown thieves?'

'Business. It's just business.' Kelly replied firmly. The gambler then walked to the sweating workmen and began handing out crisp five-dollar bills to each of them in turn.

'A little bonus for you for doing a fine job, boys. Hope you come to The Texas tonight to try your luck. Free drinks and all you can eat. Remember now that the doors will be open at six sharp.'

The satisfied men started to round up their respective tools and then slowly began to wander away. None of them knew that the money they had just been given would not last long once they entered the gambling hall later that day.

The gunman walked to the shoulder of the gambler and leaned close to the man's ear. 'What's going on, Texas Jack? You never needed no bank-robbing varmints on the payroll before.'

'I don't need bank robbers on the payroll now, Fargo.'

Fargo was frustrated and it showed in every sinew of the man's large frame. 'I heard tell that them Brewster boys are pretty handy with their guns. Is that it? You want more guns?'

'Nope,' Kelly answered swiftly. 'I got me all the gunmen I need, Fargo. Besides how good with a gun does any man have to be that robs banks? Any fool can run into a bank with a bandanna over his mouth waving a hogleg and scare yella-belly bank-tellers witless.'

Fargo looked down the long street at Brewster's horse once again. 'I don't get it, boss. There ain't no sense in sending for folks like the Brewster brothers. They're trouble.'

'Take it easy, *amigo*. There ain't nothing for you to fret about, Fargo.' Kelly glanced into the face of the hardened killer. 'When the time's right, I'll tell you everything you need to know. What you have to do.'

'What are you gonna tell me to do, Texas Jack?' Fargo looked even more confused.

'What do I normally tell you to do, Fargo?' Kelly pulled out his golden pocket watch and flipped its gleaming lid open. He nodded to himself, then returned the timepiece to his hand-tailored silk vest pocket. 'Tell me, what is it that you do better than anyone else?'

A smile came to the gunslinger's face. He nodded and then drew both his guns faster than most men could even blink. 'You want me to kill that thief?'

Kelly did not answer. His calculating eyes simply watched the expert killer twirl both weapons on his index fingers before slipping the matched pair of .45s back into their holsters.

There was no expression upon the gambler's face as he chewed the end of his cigar. After a slight nod, Texas Jack patted the side of the gunslinger's unshaven face, then turned on his heels and headed towards his gleaming gambling-palace and the rest of his hired men.

'C'mon! Let's get us some whiskey down our necks, boys,' he boomed. 'We got us a busy night ahead of us and I for one ain't gonna face it sober!'

Fargo paused on the boardwalk

outside the gambling-house and again looked along Main Street at the outlaw's horse. He grinned wide, then trailed the rest of the men into the building.

6

Sundown came quickly in the blistering desert. As the fiery orb began its inevitable journey into night the sky suddenly turned the colour of fresh blood. No man-made inferno could have created such an awesome sight as a sky apparently on fire above the oasis and the solitary, brutally wounded rider who had at last managed to reach Desert Springs. Sheer willpower was the only thing that kept the horseman astride the tall muscular stallion as he steered it determinedly ever onward towards the place where he would reluctantly seek the help of other men. Iron Eyes inhaled the scent of civilization and did not like its fragrance. His blood-covered hands fumbled for a cigar which was not covered in his own gore. He found one and forced it between his cracked lips, then ran a thumbnail across a match. He inhaled the smoke but it did not ease the pain. The bounty hunter knew that death was now riding on his shoulder. It had been a constant companion throughout his entire life but now he actually seemed to be hearing its mocking voice.

You're mine, Iron Eyes, it seemed to say. I've got you this time. There's no escape from your destiny.'

Iron Eyes sucked hard on the twisted black weed, then screwed up his eyes and stared ahead. There were many people in this strange place, he told himself. He then saw a wooden marker to his right and focused upon it.

'Desert Springs,' he read.

The palomino walked steadily past the first building and Iron Eyes saw the reaction of people on its boardwalk. They all raised their hands. Some to shield their eyes from the setting sun, so as to get a better view of the horrific vision. Others simply covered their mouths to muffle their terrified groans.

Iron Eyes rode on.

Now, hours since the last of the infamous Brewster clan had ridden into Desert Springs the marshal and his deputy had returned to the small Main Street café to partake of another hot meal. A meal which would enable them to work to the early hours of the following day. But if anything was guaranteed to spoil the appetite of even the heartiest of men it was the sight of Iron Eyes as he came into view from the window of the café.

It was a stunned Monte Bale who lowered his coffee cup when he saw the bloodcurdling vision astride the tall palomino riding down the centre of Main Street. The marshal rose to his feet and wiped the corners of his mouth with a napkin.

'Good grief! What in tarnation is that?' he muttered loud enough to draw the attention of all the other diners within the small room.

An innocent smile etched the face of the deputy. He had never witnessed the expression now carved into the marshal's face.

'What's wrong, Monte?' Joshua asked as he slid the last slice of apple pie into his mouth and chewed. 'You looks like you seen a ghost.'

'Maybe I have.' Bale pulled out a silver half-dollar and placed it down next to his plate. 'Whatever that is he's sure not like any man I ever seen before.'

The seated Joshua continued to smile. 'Are you joshing with me? What you talking about, Monte?'

'That!'

Hastily the deputy got to his feet, turned and looked out of the window to where his superior was staring in disbelief. When he too set eyes upon the bounty hunter he gasped.

'Oh deary me! What in the name of my aunt Bessie is that, Marshal?'

'He got an arrow in him, whatever he is, Joshua.' Bale picked up his hat from the chair next to him, placed it on his head and made his way to the door. 'C'mon, boy!'

'Sure is our day to have us some

pitiful-looking folks visiting town, Monte,' Joshua observed as he licked the plate and then left it. 'They're getting worse-looking, though, if he's anything to go by.'

'And both coming from the desert,' Bale added, rubbing his chin thoughtfully. 'There's only one reason for two men to come from the same direction.'

Joshua nodded firmly. 'Sure is. Just one reason. Eh, what exactly would that reason be, Monte?'

'One man has to be trailing the other,' Bale answered.

'That's just what I thought,' the deputy agreed.

Both marshal and deputy stepped out beneath the porch overhang and paused for a few moments. They looked long and hard at the horseman who was swaying in the saddle as he got closer. There seemed to be no hint of life in the rider. The last rays of the sun highlighted the gore-covered figure and his magnificent mount.

'Sweet Lord!' Joshua swallowed and

rubbed his mouth on his sleeve. 'Is he alive, Monte? He sure looks deader than anything I ever seen.'

'Well, Joshua, why don't we go find out?' Bale rested a hand on the grip of his holstered gun and with his deputy at his side began to make his way across the sand to where the stallion was headed. When he was directly in the horse's path, Bale raised both arms to the handsome animal.

To their mutual surprise, Iron Eyes tilted his head up slightly and then pulled back on his reins. The stallion snorted and stopped. The gruesome bounty hunter stared down at the men with stars pinned to their chests.

'You got a sawbones in this town?' the bounty hunter asked in a low drawl. 'You might have noticed that I kinda need me some doctorin', Marshal.'

'Oh, we noticed OK.' Joshua nodded.

Bale looked at the savage bullet hole in the rider's thigh and then turned his attention to the arrow buried deep in the shoulder of the horseman. The lawman walked around the stallion and winced when he saw the arrowhead of the vicious projectile protruding out of Iron Eyes's back. Dried blood and flesh clung to the flint tip of the arrow.

'Satisfied?' Iron Eyes asked drily.

'You must have met up with some Apaches, stranger,' Bale remarked as he reached the head of the stallion once more.

'Yep!' Iron Eyes nodded.

'I thought that all the Indians in these parts were friendly,' Bale added.

A smile flashed across Iron Eyes's twisted features. 'They probably are except when they meets up with the likes of me, Marshal. I tend to bring out the bad in most folks. Indians don't cotton to me. Never have.'

'Why?'

Iron Eyes rubbed his fevered brow. 'Coz I'm Iron Eyes!'

The deputy edged closer to Bale's side. His eyes were wide and his mouth open.

'Glory be! He's alive! I read that he

was dead a couple of years back, Monte.'

Bale gritted his teeth. 'Are you really Iron Eyes?'

'What else would I be?' Iron Eyes gestured to his face and its hideous scars. 'You ever heard of another critter who looks even a little like I do, Marshal?'

'Nope,' Bale admitted.

Iron Eyes tilted his head backwards again. He inhaled deeply and yet seemed to be unable to fully fill his lungs. A shocked expression emerged through his scarred features. After what felt like an eternity the horseman managed to find his breath.

'You OK?' the deputy asked. 'You looks powerful ill, Mr Iron Eyes.'

'I bin better, boy!' Iron Eyes retorted.

Bale stepped close to the blood-soaked saddle and rested a hand on the palomino's neck. 'Who started the ruckus with them Apaches? You or them?'

'It was kinda even. They don't like me and I ain't partial to them. We just don't get on. Seems that all Indians got

72

a short fuse when they meets up with me. I was just defending myself and wasting precious bullets. I hate killing folks who ain't got bounty on their heads. Ain't no profit in it. None at all.'

'You kill them all?' Joshua asked nervously.

Iron Eyes nodded. 'Yep.'

'Why are you here, Iron Eyes?' the marshal asked, stoutly trying not to show his dread of the horrific man who swayed on his saddle above him.

A thin, bony, bloody hand forced down into one of the deep pockets of the trail coat and pulled out three crumpled Wanted posters. Iron Eyes handed them to the lawman. Bale flattened them out against the shoulder of the horse and screwed up his eyes as he digested the words printed upon them. He then looked up into the face of the man who was staring down at him.

'You after the Brewster boys?'

'Only one of them,' Iron Eyes corrected. 'Joe Brewster.'

Joshua bravely moved closer. 'Why not the other two?'

'I already done for them, sonny,' Iron Eyes spat. 'I trailed Joe right to the outskirts of this place. He must have come this way. You seen a varmint with a lotta bags full of money in the last few hours?'

Marshal Bale gave a firm nod as he pushed the posters back into the trail-coat pocket whence they had emerged only seconds earlier.'

'Yep! A stranger rode in a few hours or so back and he was laden down with hefty bags.'

Excitedly, Iron Eyes clenched both bony fists. 'Good! I got the bastard! He's mine! I knew he was close! I can smell him!'

Joshua stepped back fearfully. 'He ain't no critter, Iron Eyes. He's a man.'

Iron Eyes looked hard at the youngster. 'He's an outlaw with bounty on his head. Dead or alive, boy. That's what the posters say. He gave up being a man when he became vermin.'

'If he's wanted by the law it's my job to bring him to book, Iron Eyes,' Bale drawled. 'I don't want no bounty hunter letting rip in my town. Innocent folks could get hurt.'

'What?' A rage swept through the bounty hunter. He was about to shout down at the man standing next to his horse when he felt his head start to spin and his eyes blur. Iron Eyes began to shake as he desperately fought against the whirlpool of mist which was filling his head. Then he lost the battle and toppled.

He fell like a lifeless rag doll from his high perch.

Monte Bale caught the thin figure in his arms as both Iron Eyes's trusty Navy Colts fell from his belt into the sand.

'You be careful you don't strain yourself, Monte,' Joshua said as he hovered beside his stalwart companion and picked up the two guns. 'Hell! These guns ain't very heavy!'

'They're Navy Colts, Joshua. Just like

their owner, they don't weigh hardly anything at all. Iron Eyes is as light as a feather. No heavier than a little kid,' the marshal said.

'Is he dead, Monte?' Joshua asked nervously.

'He sure well ought to be, the amount of blood he's lost!' The marshal swung around and began to walk as fast as his legs could manage in the direction of the doctor's office. 'C'mon! We gotta get him to Doc Hardy fast.'

'Oh glory be!' the deputy mumbled as he raced ahead of the marshal to alert the doctor that he had a new client.

Within a minute the marshal had reached the door of the doctor's office and entered after Joshua. Doc Hardy was a man who would never see sixty again and sat at his desk rubbing his whiskers, as all men of that age tend to do. He watched as the powerful lawman lay Iron Eyes's limp body down on his side on top of the long padded table so that the arrow was not broken off prematurely.

'C'mon, Doc!' Joshua urged the medical man until he got to his feet. 'We got you a patient here.'

Hardy ambled towards the horrific sight, and then gave out a long sigh. He had seen many victims of violence in his time in the West but none quite as bad as what lay before him now. He took his eyeglasses from his coat pocket and placed them on the end of his nose.

He shook his head sadly. 'What you bring him here for? The undertaker's down the street a ways, Monte! What you bring him here for? This pitiful soul is dead!'

'I knew he was a gonner.' Joshua sniffed and looked at the bounty hunter's guns in his hands.

Bale moved closer to the motionless bounty hunter. 'He ain't dead, Doc. I could feel his heart pounding as I carried him here. Iron Eyes ain't dead.'

'This is Iron Eyes?' Hardy raised his bushy eye-brows, then gripped the nearer of the still man's wrists. His fingers found a pulse and his jaw dropped.

'Well, Doc?' Joshua pressed.

Hardy dragged his coat off and began rolling up his shirt sleeves.

'Damn it all! You're right, Monte. He ain't dead! Don't ask me how but Iron Eyes is somehow still alive!'

7

Darkness enveloped Desert Springs beneath its canopy of black velvet and crystal-clear stars. There was no moon and that suited the outlaw as he walked down the back stairs of the hotel and went out into the shadows. Now clad in well-tailored town attire and fresh from bathing, the clean-shaven Joe Brewster barely resembled the dishevelled rider who had ridden in to the remote settlement only five hours earlier. That suited the man as he moved unseen and unheard across the hotel's yard and into a lane which led toward the busy main thoroughfare. The closer he got to the main street the louder the town's noises became to his alert ears.

When he reached the corner of the hotel Brewster paused and placed a cigar into his mouth. His cold, merciless eyes watched a man lighting in succession the lanterns atop their tall wooden poles. With the light from countless stores cascading out on to the street it was quickly becoming a place devoid of shadows. The outlaw scratched a match down a wall and cupped its flame in his hands. He inhaled the smoke and then proceeded on to the boardwalk beneath the overhead canopy. Brewster rested a shoulder against an upright and studied the scene carefully.

The main street seemed to be even busier now than it had been during the hours of daylight. Riders seemed to be heading in both directions with an urgency that Brewster failed to comprehend. He sucked hard on the cigar and then tossed the match at the sand which had already started to dust up his new boots.

A stagecoach thundered away from the stage depot and travelled the length of the street quickly as its driver lashed the backs of his four-horse team with a bullwhip. The interior of the coach was empty. It seemed that people came to Desert Springs but few left.

The outlaw turned his head and glanced up the street. His gaze focused upon the building he had been seeking. He had heard that the gambling-house was being constructed when he and his brothers had set out on their last job. Now it was completed and open for business.

Flaming torches had been erected all around the entrance of the gambling-hall. Their light illuminated the façade of the freshly painted structure.

'The Texas House.' Brewster whispered through a line of grey smoke. 'Mighty fine-looking!'

With skilled hands he checked his gunbelt and the guns it carried. Both safety loops were pulled off the gun hammers by the man whose eyes never left their target. A thought crept into his mind about the two hefty bags in his room. He patted his left pants leg pocket and felt the key he had used to secure the room's lock. The outlaw's thoughts then quickly returned to the street before him: the long street with the brightly illuminated edifice at its end.

He watched the crowds of men.

Joe Brewster was well-used to watching streets. He had done it for most of his adult life. It had been his job to study many streets whilst his two brothers had entered banks and robbed them of most of their assets. He would remain mounted and clear streets of any possible dangers to his more ruthless brothers, buying them enough time to mount up and ride. Yet unlike his siblings, Joe Brewster was an expert shot with both pistol and Winchester. His skill had saved their lives many times by picking off lawmen and ambitious townsfolk alike.

But now he was alone.

Alone to finish the job they had started. Doubts filled his mind as to the logic of what Clem and Frank had arranged with Kelly but he was willing to see it through. Would Texas Jack honour his promise? Would he? A gnawing in his innards told him the opposite.

The outlaw dropped the cigar next to the spent match. He crushed it with his boot heel before setting off towards the place which seemed to be attracting scores of men like moths to a naked flame.

Brewster did not want to gamble or partake in the pleasures of the imported females who would fill the upper floor of the newly constructed edifice. He had another reason to head to The Texas House.

A more important reason.

One which Texas Jack Kelly was well aware of.

It was a long walk to The Texas House. Yet Brewster was in no rush. If the outlaw had any nerves they were well disguised and totally under control. For the first time in his entire career Brewster was without the support of his siblings. Frank and Clem had always made the decisions and Joe had followed their lead. It had been Clem who had arranged the meeting with Texas Jack nearly four months earlier, but now it would be the only surviving member of the gang who would actually encounter the mysterious gambler.

It seemed as though no one even noticed the outlaw as he moved gradually towards the gambling-house. He remained on the opposite side of the street as he gradually approached the flaming torches.

Then a man who had obviously drunk more than his ration of hard liquor staggered towards the outlaw. His neat clothing was stained with vomit and other even less fragrant substances. At first Joe Brewster was amused. Then he realized that of all the eyes in Desert Springs he had walked up to a pair which recognized him.

'It's you!' the drunk slurred. 'You! You dirty low-down robber!'

Brewster moved up to a wall and rested in its shadow, but the man with the pointing finger closed in on him like a well-trained cutting horse. He jabbed each word into the outlaw's chest.

'You stole every penny I had back in Waco two years back, you bastard!' the man shouted.

Men lived a lot longer when honest folks failed to notice them. Brewster intended to continue living. He glanced all around him at the crowd. They had not heard the words and Brewster knew he had to prevent any further outbursts from reaching their ears.

He crossed the wide street as horsemen steered their mounts towards The Texas House but the drunk kept snapping at his heels, ranting.

'Turn around, you bastard! I know it's you!'

Brewster hurriedly slid behind a buckboard as a burly man piled provisions from a grocery store on the flatbed. He stepped up on to the boardwalk and pretended to look at the goods inside the window for a few seconds. The drunk caught up with him, grabbed his arm and pulled him around.

Their eyes met.

'Git going!' Brewster snarled.

'I ain't going anywhere!' the man raved. 'I got money in the bank here now and you ain't gonna go helping yourself to that as well. Savvy?'

'I savvy.' The outlaw grabbed the man's throat. He squeezed it, then frogmarched the drunk around a corner into the blackness.

It took less than thirty seconds for Brewster silently to kill the man. His strong hands crushed the throat until there were no more words. The body went limp and fell into the sand. Brewster left it there and returned to the street. The night had not brought any lowering in the temperature and beads of sweat traced their way down from the band of his new hat and over his freshly shaven face.

Again he checked his guns. They were loaded and ready.

People continued to move up and

down the wooden walkway as more and more streetlights were ignited. The aroma of coal tar filled his nostrils as he tilted his head and stared down towards the gambling-hall.

His eyes ignored the patrons who were being allowed in through its gleaming doors. His attention was on the heavily armed men who appeared to be in charge of things. Brewster rubbed his lips as his body turned toward The Texas House. He began to walk. Walk slowly.

Each step was calculated.

His honed bank robber's instincts were now in operation. He was not foolhardy enough simply to walk to the front door of the building and ask to see Texas Jack Kelly. That was as dumb as walking up to a bank and asking if he might rob it.

Brewster paused every few steps.

His eyes darted to every movement whether it be of man or beast.

He absorbed everything and tried to work out whether his brothers had made such a good deal with Kelly as they had all first assumed it to be. Gamblers were lowlife. Their entire lives were devoted to cheating and stealing.

Texas Jack Kelly also had a reputation for using his many hired gunmen to kill as well. Brewster was now within spitting distance of the porch overhang of the large brightly decorated building. The flaming torches' light danced across the glossy paintwork and its many glass windows.

It was a dazzling sight but it failed to impress the outlaw.

Brewster searched his pockets for a cigar as he counted the armed men who guarded the building as they allowed eager men through their ranks.

He placed another cigar between his lips. His eyes looked up the alley to the nearer side of The Texas House. He could just make out another of the hired gunslingers lurking at a side door halfway along the the long wall. Joe Brewster struck a match and inhaled his cigar's smoke as he started to walk again. He did not head to where all the other men were going. He continued on until he was able to stop again and give the other side of the building a searching look. There was no door on this long wall. No door and therefore no man standing guard.

A horseman rode close to the well-dressed outlaw and Brewster used that moment to slip unseen into the alley. He continued to smoke his cigar as he paced along the side of the building until he reached the rear yard.

Brewster rested at the corner and removed his hat before bending slightly forward to look at the rear of The Texas house. A door was placed in the middle of the back wall with a lantern above it.

Another of Kelly's henchmen guarded it. He had counted six so far. Each one of them packing more firepower than most men would ever require.

The outlaw nodded knowingly, placed his hat back on his head and then turned around. He retraced his steps back to the main street and this time went to where all the other men were heading.

He pulled out a swollen wallet as he approached the guards who, upon seeing the wad of bills, ushered him into the gambling-house.

Joe Brewster returned his wallet to his inside pocket and looked around the impressive interior. No expense had been spared in making this the grandest building of its kind in southern Texas, Brewster thought.

It was crowded.

That suited him just fine.

Again the outlaw smiled. A dozen or more near-naked females suddenly appeared at the top of the elaborate staircase. What clothing they were wearing suited the temperature and their profession.

Brewster diverted his stare from the handsome women and then caught sight of a man who, like the building itself, appeared to be adorned with the very best and most expensive decoration. A gold tiepin with a thumbnail-sized diamond moved through the crowds like a king amid peasants.

The outlaw knew that, although Kelly knew what his brothers looked like, he had never set eyes on the man who was no moving freely through the various rooms unhindered.

Joe Brewster was again invisible.

Again he smiled.

8

Sundown had not brought any rest to the silver-haired medical man. There was no wandering along Main Street to the grand opening of The Texas House for Wilfred Eli Hardy. Doc Hardy had laboured through what had remained of the long afternoon and into the early hours of darkness on the strange, emaciated creature who, Marshal Bale had informed him, was the legendary bounty hunter Iron Eyes. Yet for all his labours it felt to the seasoned sawbones that he was working on a corpse. He had in fact seen many dead men who displayed more animation than Iron Eyes was that day. Not a muscle had twitched on the limp bounty hunter since Bale had placed his wounded body down on the doctor's table. The only hint that Iron Eyes was actually alive was the fevered droplets of sweat which trailed from every pore in his face, scalp and body. The table was soaked in it.

It had been relatively easy to clean and patch up the hole in the bounty hunter's leg and a few well-placed stitches had stemmed the flow of blood quickly. Not that Hardy believed that it was due to his own medical skill, but more to the fact that he could barely see how there could be any blood remaining in the painfully lean frame.

Whatever kept Iron Eyes alive it certainly was not in any medical book that he had ever read. Perhaps it was sheer stubbornness or maybe it was true that this strange monster of a man was not really alive at all. Everything Hardy had ever learned about his profession was being mocked by Iron Eyes's refusal to die. There was no way that any living creature on God's earth could remain alive after such an incredible loss of blood, but the bounty hunter was alive.

Perhaps God had nothing to do with

this pitiful being, Hardy had considered hours earlier. Maybe it was Satan himself who had created Iron Eyes in his own image.

Hardy had vainly tried not to look at the face or body of the man who lay atop his table as he attended to the injuries. Yet the scars were like magnets to an iron rod. They drew his attention and curiosity over and over again. How could anyone survive such injuries? Most of the old scars told the wily old man that Iron Eyes must have tended his own wounds many times. Crudely stitched scars more akin to saddlework than mending broken human flesh were everywhere. His entire body was like a patchwork bed-throw. Brutal reminders such as burned and melted flesh also showed Hardy that the red-hot blade of a knife, or a poker, had been used many times to stem the flow of blood in the past.

Hardy knew only too well that it took a man with unimaginable courage to cauterize his own wounds in that way.

Most men would die of heart failure brought about by the shock but not this creature. Iron Eyes had survived.

But of all the injuries the near-naked body displayed it was those on the face that horrified Hardy the most. When the matted mane of long black hair had been pushed off the face it revealed something more gruesome even than Hardy's own wildest nightmares. It was the most terrifying image he had ever set eyes upon.

Despite this, Hardy had forged on. One of the bounty hunter's eyes had an untreated scar which made it impossible for the lid to close, leaving the eye always half-open. The eye appeared to watch his every movement. There was evidence of bullet scars across the top and sides of the head which had left hairless tracks through the otherwise thick hair. Half of one ear had been shot off. The mouth was twisted where yet again more wounds had been left to mend themselves and had done so badly.

One cheekbone was obviously crushed beneath the eye which could not close, giving Iron Eyes the look of someone who, even while unconscious, was continually snarling.

Every few moments Doc Hardy had checked his patient's pulse to persuade himself to continue working on what appeared to be a corpse. When he had completed work on the leg wound he moved to the more difficult injury.

The arrow which had gone right through Iron Eyes's shoulder presented a more problematic task. The old doctor had seen many similar wounds in his earlier days, when Indian attacks were more common, but none for more than a decade. He knew there was a trick to removing the deadly projectiles from a man without tearing vital arteries apart. One false move and the razor-sharp arrowhead would simply sever anything in its path as it was withdrawn, leaving the patient to bleed internally. He had seen men pull arrows from their bodies quite easily and then die of unseen haemorrhaging.

The arrow had to be carefully broken into two sections and each part then carefully extracted, from front and back. The chances of poisoning were high and that probably accounted for the fever his sweat-soaked patient had been displaying, Hardy told himself. He knew that Apaches had a knowledge of wild plants and poisons such as he himself would never acquire. The archer who had sent this arrow into Iron Eyes was probably a hunter and therefore the flint arrowhead must have been treated with something which would render whatever it hit unconscious. But Iron Eyes had been conscious when he rode into Desert Springs, Hardy thought. Bale had told him so. Again, Hardy shook his head in bewilderment.

Hardy had carefully studied the arrow when he first set to work. It was an old piece of wood. Not rotten but close. Damn close. Age had stained its length with a green mould, a fine powder of potentially deathly spores, a lot of which was inside Iron Eyes.

The medical man had known from the outset that it would take every ounce of his knowledge and deftness to save the bounty hunter's life. After hours of careful preparation Doc Hardy knew that he had to extract the arrow and then somehow purify the hole left in its gruesome wake. A hole which went right through Iron Eyes.

There were several ways of achieving this, but which of them, he pondered, was the best? After a few moments he decided to use whiskey and a long waxed taper to sterilize the hole. He knew that good liquor poked through a savage hole would kill most germs.

If done incorrectly, it had also been known to kill the patient almost immediately.

Doc Hardy opened his rolltop desk and pulled out an almost full bottle of labelled Scotch. He placed it on the table next to his patient's head. He removed its cork and took a swig before resuming his work. It seemed a sorrowful waste of good whiskey to use it on someone who looked to be hanging on to life by a thread.

He dragged a stool close to the table, rested his rump upon it and leaned closer to his patient. He had already managed to cut the tail of the arrow away and discard it on to his blood-stained floor. Every now and then he found his eyes drawn to the Apache feathered flight. It reminded him of the early days when he had first ventured into the wilds of southern Texas. Then there had been many branches of the Apache family. So many that it was impossible to number them all. But that had been when his hair had not been white, when he had a spring in his legs and not a stiffening creak. Now the Apaches were as rare as the once abundant nomadic buffalo to the north. Their numbers now were a pitiful reminder of what the settlers had done to a once noble race.

Sweat flowed from the brow of the

old man like a ceaseless waterfall. It nearly equalled that which oozed from Iron Eyes. When shadows had at last overwhelmed the light inside his office, his shaking fingers had managed to light all his lamps. Hardy had arranged them as close to the motionless Iron Eyes as possible before proceeding with his task.

It had been a slow process. The sticky flesh had clung to the shaft of the arrow and almost sapped Hardy's strength as he tried to extract the part of the arrow which protruded out of Iron Eyes's back. After what felt like a lifetime the arrow came free and with it a trickle of blood, which he plugged with clean rags. Soaked in his own sweat the old man had dragged his stool around to the front of the bounty hunter and gazed again at the face which appeared to be looking straight back at him.

A million thoughts crept through his tired brain.

One of which was: was Iron Eyes actually able to see him even though he was totally unconscious?

The thought chilled him as he had continued on with his work and gripped the tail of the arrow with pliers more suited to extracting teeth.

Hardy had tugged and tugged. His concern for not causing even more damage inside the motionless creature on the table had slowed his progress drastically. Then, after what had become a battle between the medical man and the defiant arrow, he decided that he had to forget his worries and get the last of the projectile out of Iron Eyes so that he could tend to the severe injury inside the sleeping man.

If there was poison in the man he had to kill it before it killed Iron Eyes. That could only be achieved after the wooden shaft was dragged out of the body.

Mustering every ounce of his strength Doc Hardy had raised a knee, placed it against the flat belly of the bounty hunter and then pulled with all his might. Twisting and turning his old arms as they gripped the pliers firmly Doc Hardy began to curse to gods he no longer believed in. Then he had given out a grunt and the defiant arrow finally succumbed. The stool went hurtling away from beneath him. Hardy found himself a yard away from the table with the pliers in his hands and the bloody shaft of wood gripped between their pincers.

'Got ya!' he yelled triumphantly.

He tossed the pliers aside, then rushed to his patient and bent down. He closed one eye and squinted into the hole. It looked bad, real bad.

Blood was now flowing from the fresh hole. Iron Eyes was bleeding inside from torn veins, or worse. Hardy ran his bloody hands through his white hair and tried to think through his own exhaustion.

'Come on! Think, you old fool!' he shouted to himself. 'He's bleeding inside and you gotta stop it. Can't go sticking in a poker from the pot-belly stove in there, although I reckon that's what he'd do to himself. Nope! There gotta be . . . '

Hardy paused, then clapped his hands together.

A revelation swept over him. He grabbed hold of the whiskey bottle and the taper. He placed the bottle closer to the chest of his patient and tore a strip of cloth from the tail of his own shirt. He carefully wrapped it around the taper and soaked it in the whiskey before pushing the taper in and out of the wound from both front and back of the prostrate Iron Eyes.

When satisfied that he had filled the hole with as much whiskey as it was possible to get into the bounty hunter he raised his arm above the nearest of his lamps. The taper's wick ignited like a fire cracker.

'I sure hope this works, Iron Eyes!' Hardy muttered as he placed the burning taper close to the bounty hunter's whiskey-soaked chest wound.

A flash temporarily blinded the doctor. He staggered backwards, then blinked hard. The flaming liquor had gone right through Iron Eyes from front to back. Smoke drifted upwards towards his ceiling as Hardy ventured back to his patient. The acrid stench of burning flesh filled the old man's nostrils but the bleeding had stopped.

Doc Hardy carefully rolled the bounty hunter over until Iron Eyes was on his back. The doctor rubbed his dry mouth and then took another swig from his bottle. The whiskey tasted good.

Hardy's fingers carefully picked up his patient's thin bony wrist. Suddenly the smile left his triumphant features.

He could not find a pulse.

Hardy raised his hand and pressed his fingers into the neck of the man who lay as still as death itself. Again there was no sign of a heartbeat. He rushed around the table and lowered his head on to the blood-and-sweat-covered chest. Hard though he strained Hardy could detect no sign of a heartbeat.

The old man looked as sick as Iron

Eyes, his face drawn and almost as white as his hair.

'Damn it all, boy! We was almost there! What you have to up and quit now for?'

Just at that moment the door to his office opened and Monte Bale entered with his hat carefully gripped in his hands. Hardy glanced up at the marshal. He acknowledged him with a nod.

'Monte!'

'Any news, Doc?' Bale asked.

'Yep, I got news, Monte,' Hardy sighed and then sat down on the chair next to his desk. He held his whiskey bottle in his hands and stared at its amber contents.

Bale ventured another step closer. 'What news, Doc?'

'Iron Eyes is dead.'

'Dead?'

Hardy nodded. 'Yep.'

After these few words had sunk into both men's minds there was a silence which lingered for what each silently felt was a lifetime. The tall lawman closed the door behind him and ventured across the room towards the stony-faced doctor. He rested a hand briefly on the thin shoulder, then paced to where the body lay. Monte Bale had also seen death many times in his career while wearing a tin star, but it still did not sit well with him.

His narrowed eyes drifted up and down the scarred creature who lay amid sweat and blood. It looked as though the bounty hunter could have died a hundred times before this. Most of the injuries were bad enough to have been fatal. Fatal to any normal man.

Nearly naked, Iron Eyes looked even less human.

Monte Bale rubbed a large hand across his face. He tried to take in the brutal wounds which covered the emaciated body. If there was a bit of the bounty hunter which had not been shot, cut or burned in the past it was impossible to find it in the lamplight. Bale turned the lamp's brass wheels and lowered the illumination around the table as if in respect to the corpse.

He, like everyone else in the West, had heard about Iron Eyes and thought the stories were all a tad tall. Seeing what the bounty hunter must have endured through his life made the marshal realize that they were probably all true.

Sighing, Bale turned and looked back at the doctor. Hardy was staring with glazed eyes into the far wall. The marshal knew that there were few men who were better at his job than this old-timer. Only age had slowed him, not lack of skill.

'You got a blanket around here, Doc?' Bale asked drily. 'I thought I'd cover him up.'

Hardy gestured at the couch beneath the window where he often slept when too weary to go to his bed.

'Use that 'un, Monte,' Hardy said. 'It needs a wash anyway!'

Bale strode to the couch, lifted the white sheet up and then returned to the long table. He carefully covered the body and then rubbed his neck thoughtfully.

'What happened? It looks like you fixed up his wounds just fine, Doc.'

Hardy gave a slight shrug. 'Beats me. I thought we were doing fine but I had to burn the poison out from the wound left in him when I extracted that damn filthy arrow. He must have not had the strength to cope with the shock.'

Bale shook his head. 'By all accounts this man was the lowest of the low, but anyone who lived his kinda life deserves better than dying on a table. Reckon we all gotta go somehow, though.'

There were tears in Hardy's eyes when his head turned and he looked up at the marshal.

'Damn it all, I did my best! I don't like losing patients at the best of times but when you got some critter like him dying it hurts, Monte. It hurts bad. That man or whatever he was must have lived in pain from all them old injuries for years. I figure he must have bin carrying at least a half dozen chunks of rifle or gun lead in him when he got here. That boy suffered more pain than we'll ever know. He shouldn't be dead. If he could handle that he ought to have bin able to handle what I done to him.'

'Maybe it was his time,' Bale said. 'His time to go.'

'It ought to have bin his time to die years back.'

Bale moved back to the old man. 'Why don't you and me head on over to the Silver Bell and have us some drinks, Doc? A few cool beers will wash the taste of this out of our mouths.'

'That's a good idea.' Hardy nodded and carefully rose to his feet. He placed the bottle of whiskey on his desk and walked over to where his coat was hanging. 'The fresh air will do me good. The beer will do me even more good!'

'You leaving the bottle?' Bale smiled coyly.

Hardy glanced at the bottle. 'Maybe I'll have me a few glasses of that when I get back after I've filled my innards with beer!'

Both men's attention were drawn to the office door by a gentle rapping. Bale looked at the door and his hand rested instinctively on his gun grip.

'You expecting somebody, Doc?'

Hardy pulled his half-hunter from his vest pocket and looked at its reliable hands. 'Seven sharp! Must be Beulah from the café with my evening vittles. Come on in, Beulah dear.'

Reluctantly the female turned the doorknob and ventured into the room. Word had spread like wildfire through Desert Springs about the inhuman creature whom the marshal had taken to be treated by Hardy. She averted her eyes away from the table, walked towards the two men and placed the tray down on the desk. Whatever was beneath the chequered napkin it sure smelled good.

'Now you make sure you eat this before you go to bed, Doc.'

Hardy smiled at the shapely female

who was somewhere in her mid-thirties.

'I will eat it before going to bed later on, Beulah. I promise.'

The woman left the office as quickly as her feet would carry her and closed the door firmly. Bale went to lift the edge of the napkin when Hardy slapped the back of the lawman's hand.

'Come on, Monte! Let's get out of here!'

Bale put his hat back on and glanced at the body now covered with a white sheet as he headed to the door. He gripped the handle and turned it.

'What about Iron Eyes, Doc?'

'Reckon he'll keep for a couple of hours, boy,' Hardy replied. 'I'll take me a walk down to old Perkins at the funeral parlour later and get him to come pick him up at his convenience!'

As the marshal led his companion out into the fresh air he patted the old shoulder again. 'You don't have to go marching all over town, Doc. I'll send Joshua. He needs the exercise.'

Hardy sniffed as he closed the door behind him. 'Good enough.'

9

Men cut from Joe Brewster's kind of cloth seldom made mistakes unless they were the fatal kind. The outlaw had vowed that if anyone was going to make such a mistake this night, it would not be him. He had somehow managed to move unhindered through the various levels of The Texas House whilst accepting free drinks and helping himself to the ample supply of freshly prepared food. In order not to arouse any suspicions Brewster had placed a few token bets at the roulette table before heading up the flight of stairs to where he had seen Texas Jack and Fargo head thirty minutes earlier.

He knew that they had now had plenty of time to settle down in Kelly's office and imagine their rewards when the night's takings were tallied up. All the outlaw had to do was find that

office and make his unexpected intro-
ductions.

When he reached the landing three
females draped in smiles and very little
else surrounded him. Their perfume
was enough to sober up the drunkest of
men. Brewster allowed their lips to
leave their paint on his shaven face and
their hands to grope his freshly bathed
body through his new clothes. As they
caressed him with eager fingers his keen
eyes darted from one door after another
until they found what he had been
looking for. Right at the very end of the
corridor he saw the one door which did
not have a number, just the word
'private' emblazoned upon its gleaming
surface.

Brewster handed out silver dollars to
the females and vaguely promised he
would return to them to pursue their
obvious pleasures later. With the coins
in their hands the ladies sought out new
potential clients.

The outlaw walked down the corridor towards the door. His steps being

muffled by the plush carpet, he reached it unheard in a matter of seconds.

Brewster pushed his coat tails over the holstered guns and gritted his teeth. In one fluid action he had opened the door and entered before the occupants of the room had even realized anyone was there.

Texas Jack Kelly was sitting behind his desk in a chair fit of a king. Few thrones could have equalled it. Fargo was resting his hip on the edge of the desk. Both men had glasses in their hands when they looked up.

Their startled expressions amused the bank robber.

Fargo lifted his weight to stand as Brewster drew both his weapons and cocked their hammers.

'I'd stay exactly where you are, Fargo,' the outlaw advised.

'You know me?' Fargo asked.

Brewster simply nodded.

Kelly placed his glass on his blotter and leaned back against the padded back of his chair. A smile as wide as a canyon filled his face.

'If it ain't little Joey Brewster!' He laughed.

Brewster did not see the joke. 'I'd be careful about how you talk to me, Texas Jack. I got me a real bad side and only a plumb loco fool would want to see it!'

The gambler nodded. 'I apologize, Mr Brewster. Where's Clem and Frank?'

'Dead.' The outlaw snapped a reply. 'You're dealing with me now. Savvy?'

Kelly nodded. 'I savvy.'

'How'd Clem and Frank die, Joe?' Fargo looked as curious as his question implied. 'Did you have trouble with that last bank job?'

'Nope,' Brewster replied. 'That went sweet and easy. We got what we went into that bank to get. Our trouble came a little later.'

Fargo turned on his hip. 'What kinda trouble could get the better of Clem and Frank?'

'We had a run-in with Iron Eyes,' Brewster replied. He walked across the room towards the two men who, he knew, would kill him as quickly as he would kill them given half a chance.

'Iron Eyes?' Kelly repeated the name and leaned forward. He rested his elbows on the desk and stared up at the man with the pair of Colts in his hands. 'He's in town, Joe. Did you happen to know that?'

'What?' Suddenly Brewster's expression changed. 'He's here already?'

Fargo smiled. 'You look a little sickly there, Joe. You scared of that bounty hunter?'

The outlaw swallowed hard. 'That critter is dangerous. He killed my brothers and nearly done for me. He's been following me all the way from Mexico.'

Kelly smiled again. 'Relax! My spies tell me that he's close to death. The marshal had to carry him to old Doc Hardy's place earlier this evening.'

Brewster blinked hard. 'How come?'

'He tangled with some Apaches and they sure got the better of him by all accounts.' Fargo nodded and then laughed.

'He had an arrow in him,' Kelly added. 'Leastways, that's what my spies told me.'

The outlaw was now at the desk. One gun was aimed straight at Kelly and the other at Fargo. Sweat dripped from beneath his hatband as the fear of encountering the bounty hunter again swept over him.

'Our deal will never happen as long as Iron Eyes is still breathing, Texas Jack,' Brewster said in a low, cold tone. 'He'll ruin everything for all of us.'

Kelly looked at the younger man long and hard. 'What would you suggest we do?'

'If you had any brains you'd send some of your boys to that doctor's place and kill Iron Eyes,' Brewster advised. 'That varmint is like a leech! He don't quit! Send some men to make sure he's dead, Texas Jack.'

Kelly looked at the fearful man. 'But I'm told he's as good as dead, Joe.'

'He don't die like regular folks,' the outlaw shouted. 'If you don't kill him he'll probably kill all of us.'

Fargo raised an eyebrow. 'But he only goes after men with bounty on their heads. Men like you.'

Joe Brewster looked at Fargo, then diverted his eyes to Kelly. A knowing smile etched across his face. 'You telling me that neither of you has any paper on you? There ain't no reward posters out there some-place with your faces on them?'

Both Kelly and Fargo looked concerned.

'You might have changed your names but he'll figure it. Iron Eyes don't ever forget a face he's seen on a poster. No matter how old it is, he'll recall it. He'll even know how much you're both worth dead. And that's the only way he collects.'

Kelly snapped his fingers. 'Fargo! Take Layne, Smith and Green with you to Doc Hardy's office! Kill that bounty hunter and whoever else happens to get in the way!'

Fargo looked at Brewster. 'Is it OK with you if'n I do what Texas Jack wants, Joe?'

The outlaw nodded. 'Get going. But make sure you kill him, Fargo.'

Kelly watched the door close behind Fargo, then stared up at the bank robber. He pulled a cigar from a silver box, bit off its tip and spat it away. 'Now to business, Joe. The deal I had with Clem was that you boys would bring me a bag of fresh-minted golden eagles and I'd pay you twenty-five cents on the dollar. Have you got them?'

'It was fifty cents on the dollar and I've got them!' Brewster answered as his companion struck a match and raised it to the expensive smoke. 'I got me plenty of them. Half-eagles as well.'

'I'll take every one of them for fifty cents on the dollar, Joe.' Texas Jack could not hide his eagerness at laying his hands on so much gold coin. He sucked in the smoke from his cigar and allowed it to trail from his lips. 'With my connections in the gambling-halls across southern Texas I'll be able to turn those eagles into hard cash faster than a fly can find a ripe outhouse.'

Joe Brewster continued to hold his guns at hip height.

'Don't you trust me, Joe?' Kelly asked.

The bank robber walked to the door, opened it carefully and checked the corridor. He glanced back.

'Nope. I don't trust you, Texas Jack.'

Kelly watched the man leave his office. He tapped the ash from his cigar into a glass tray and nodded to himself.

'You got brains, Joe.'

10

There was a spring in the step of Joe Brewster when he left The Texas House and walked between the lines of men who were anxious to get into the gambling-hall.

The lanterns and torches bathed the outlaw in their flickering light as he hurriedly made his way back in the direction of the hotel. For the first time since he had started out for the gambling-hall earlier that evening Brewster was confident. He knew that all he had to do was deliver the two large bags of coins into the hands of Texas Jack Kelly and he would be able to leave Desert Springs a very wealthy man.

A billfold full of crisp one-hundred-dollar bills was a lot easier to carry than the hefty gold coins he had toiled with for so many weeks that he had lost count.

But Brewster should have remained alert. He should have kept his habit of always looking over his shoulder that his elder brothers had taught him. Then perhaps he might have noticed the four heavily armed men who watched his every move from the safety and protection of the shadows close to the hotel. A quartet of men ready to dish out death because they had been told to do so by their wealthy boss.

Fargo might have agreed to go to Doc Hardy's place and ensure that Iron Eyes was actually dead, but he had had earlier instructions from his employer. Instructions which he and three of Kelly's henchmen would execute along with the bank robber before they made their way down to where they knew Iron Eyes was. First things first. The bounty hunter could wait, the small fortune in golden eagles could not. Kelly wanted that in his safe because he had never intended paying any of the Brewster brothers a red cent for it.

The sharp-eyed Fargo leaned back

until the shadows cloaked him. He looked at Jed Green, Seth Smith and Ben Layne beside him and gave a simple nod. They knew what that meant. Guns were slid from holsters and made ready.

All four men clutched a pistol in their hands as Brewster reached the board-walk outside the Desert Hotel and entered its open doors.

'Let's give our pal a visit, boys!' Fargo drawled.

There was a sound of subdued laughter as the four men curled around the corner and raced to the hotel. Fargo reached the doorway first. Brewster was about to start up the staircase when he saw them. Instinctively his hands went to go for the holstered guns beneath the tails of his new coat. They stopped when he looked straight down the barrel of Fargo's cocked Peacemaker.

'You bastard!' Brewster growled.

The four men surrounded and disarmed Brewster swiftly as Fargo pushed the barrel of his gun into the face of the bank robber and plucked the key from the outlaw's hand.

'Room three.' Fargo smiled. 'Lead the way, Joey boy!'

* * *

The old man had not enjoyed any of the three glasses of beer he had consumed whilst sitting with Marshal Bale in the heart of the near-empty saloon. Even not having had to pay for any of them had not made them taste any better. To Doc Hardy it was impossible to forget the fact that he had failed a fellow man. All his knowledge and experience had amounted to nothing yet again. These were things which all medical practitioners learned to accept if they wished to remain doctors. It was still a very bitter pill to swallow even for the most seasoned of souls, though. Death would eventually defeat even the greatest of them. Some thought that it was attempting to cheat death itself if you dared to interfere with the course of nature. To give a simple tonic might be seen as interfering with some divine purpose, and yet men still tried to save those who were sick.

They tried to help. For them there was no other course that their lives could ever take. They tried to postpone Death's inevitable victory over mere mortals.

Apart from Bale and Hardy and the bartender the Silver Bell saloon was virtually empty. It seemed the same with all the other drinking- and gambling-holes in town. The draw of the new Texas House had proved too hard to resist.

'This beer tastes like dishwater, Monte,' Hardy complained.

'Mine was just fine, Doc.' The lawman smiled.

'Maybe it's just me, then.' Hardy sniffed.

'Maybe it is.'

Hardy looked around at the wall clock. 'Did you send Joshua to the funeral parlour like I asked?'

'Yep'

'Knowing Perkins, he'll wait until I'm asleep before he comes knocking on my door,' the doctor grumbled anxiously. 'Maybe I ought to go check that Perkins got the message. What you reckon, Monte?'

Bale stood, placed his empty beer glass down and smiled at the older man. 'No need, Doc.' Joshua came back here and told us that he had a word with Perkins and he said he'll pick up the body when he's got time. Don't you recall?'

Hardy wrinkled his eyes. 'Nope. Maybe this beer is stronger than it tastes. I must be plumb tuckered out if I forgot you telling me that.'

'You worked hard on Iron Eyes, Doc.' Bale nodded. 'Anyone would be tired.'

'Reckon so.' Doc swallowed the last of his beer and placed his glass down next to the marshal's.

'I better go do my rounds, Doc,' Bale

said. 'I'll drop in the office first, though.'

'Want company?'

Bale grinned. 'Why, sure. C'mon.'

Both men left the saloon and walked across the street towards the marshal's office. Doc Hardy pointed to the end of the street where a crowd was gathered outside The Texas House, bathed in torchlight.

'Look at them fools, Monte. Trying to get into a place guaranteed to rob them blind. All that pretty paint and a few new girls and men just turn into fish.'

'Fish?' Bale unlocked the office door, walked to the nearest of his lamps and lit its wick as the doctor made for a chair. 'Men turn into fish? Maybe I'm a bit tired as well coz I can't for the life of me see the connection.'

Hardy nodded firmly as he relaxed. 'Sure enough. You put a bit of shiny paper on a hook and drop it in a creek and what happens? Some dumb fish will up and swallow it hook, line and sinker! All that Texas Jack has done is bait a hook and look at them two-legged fish lining up to swallow it.'

'They'll even pay him for the privilege, Doc.' Bale laughed as he made his way to his desk and sat down.

Joshua was red-faced and gasping for air when he reached the marshal's office and burst in. Monte Bale looked up from his desk and frowned.

'What in tarnation is wrong, boy?'

'You OK, Joshua?' Hardy asked.

The panting deputy frantically waved his right arm around as it pointed out at the street.

'Suck in some air, Joshua.' Bale smiled. 'You'll burst otherwise.'

Joshua did as instructed, then staggered to the larger of the two desks inside the office. He placed the palms of both hands down on it and blinked hard.

'I found me a body out there, Monte!'

The smile evaporated from Bale's face. He slowly stood and walked around the desk until he was nose to nose with his red-faced deputy.

'You found a body?'

Hardy got to his feet and moved to both men. 'What kinda body did you find, boy?'

Joshua nodded. 'A dead'un!'

Bale walked to the open door and looked up and down the street. 'Where?'

'Go on, Joshua. Tell Monte where you found this body,' Hardy teased.

The deputy frowned at the doctor. 'Quit baiting me, Doc. I did find me a body. Honest.'

Bale grabbed his deputy by the arm and hauled him to the open door. 'Where did you find this body?'

'Up in the alley next to Cooper's store.' Joshua pointed.

'What were you doing up there?' Hardy enquired.

'I was having me a looksee at the new Texas House and went into the alley to relieve myself when I done fell over Lane Smith. He was just lying there all quiet like. I could smell the corn whiskey and said for him to get up and go home.'

'You sure he's dead?' Bale asked.

'Dead drunk by the sounds of it.' Hardy grinned.

'He sure is dead.' Joshua nodded hard. 'I give him a real good kicking and he just lay there all quiet like. So I bent down and turned him over. He was covered in all sorts of dirt. Shame, really, coz he had himself a darn nice suit on.'

Bale pulled his hat from the stand and wiped its band with his hand. 'But he's dead? You're sure that he's dead?'

'How many times have I gotta tell you boys, Monte? He's deader than my Aunt Bessie.'

Bale nodded and stepped out on to the boardwalk. 'I never heard any gunfire.'

Joshua waved his arms around. 'He weren't shot none. Leastways if'n he was I didn't see no blood. I struck a match and held it under his chin and it looked all messed up. Bruised an' all.'

Doc Hardy rubbed his whiskers. 'Sounds like he was strangled, Monte.'

The marshal gritted his teeth. 'Go get the undertaker, Joshua!'

The deputy blushed. 'Can I go to the outhouse first? You see I never had me time to — '

Bale nodded. 'You go and — '

Joshua turned on his heels fast. 'OK! After I've gotten rid of all this liquid in me I'll go get the undertaker.'

The doctor edged close to Bale. 'I better tag along with you to see if Lane Smith is really dead, Monte. And if he is I have to figure out what killed him. Sure sounds like he was strangled though. Who throttles a man in these parts?'

'Someone who wants to kill quiet and ain't got a knife.'

'I'll tag along.' Hardy sighed. 'I'm a little curious about this and no mistake.'

'I'll appreciate your help, Doc.' Bale looked back across his office at the open rear door. 'And put your damn gun on, Joshua.'

Hardy stood on the boardwalk with his hands in his pockets and rocked back and forth. 'Could be whiskey poisoning! Homemade corn liquor has seen off more folks around here than smallpox!'

Just at that moment Rufe Carter was crossing the street, going towards the marshal's office. He touched the brim of his hat when he saw the lawman and the doctor.

'Marshal! Doc!'

'Hey, Rufe!' Bale stepped down into the street. 'You had yourself a new customer earlier on today.'

Carter raised his eyebrows. 'I had a couple. I think it must be The Texas House opening tonight.'

'The one I'm interested in was looking real tuckered. Came riding into town from the desert.'

'Mr Brewbaker,' Carter said. 'He was in a bit of a mess when he arrived but he's looking mighty fine now! Amazing what a bath and some new clothes will do for a soul.'

Bale placed his own hat on. 'Thanks, Rufe.'

'My pleasure.' Carter carried on walking.

Hardy stepped down and caught up to the marshal. 'What was that about, Monte?'

'Rufe don't know it but he's got himself a bank robber staying in his hotel.'

'Only a bank robber could afford the prices that varmint charges.' Hardy sighed.

Both men started for Cooper's General Store.

Then a deafening salvo of gunfire rang out into Main Street. It echoed off the fronts of the buildings and rang in the ears of the two walking men.

'Where'd that come from, Monte?' Hardy asked.

Bale drew his gun and began to run. 'The hotel!'

11

With smoke billowing from the barrel of his Colt, Fargo watched as Smith and Green left the hotel room with the hefty pair of canvas bank bags between them. Ben Layne hovered next to Fargo like a vulture over the stricken Brewster. Blood had splattered across the room's far wall as evidence, if any were necessary, of what Texas Jack Kelly's top gunman had done.

Two bullets had already felled the bank robber. What remained of Brewster was crumpled beyond the bed where he had landed after being punched off his feet by the sheer force of Fargo's bullets.

'Let me finish him off?' Layne begged as his index finger twitched inside the Colt's trigger guard.

Fargo glanced at Layne. 'He's already finished, Ben. You go and tell Jed and

Seth to wait for me out back with them bags. I ain't gonna be long.'

'Who's gonna go and finish Iron Eyes off, Fargo?' Layne slid his gun back into its holster and backed off toward the door. 'I thought we was headed there after this.'

'Jed and Seth are going to kill that stinking bounty hunter, Ben. OK?' Fargo's thumb dragged the hammer of his Peacemaker back until it locked into position again. He raised the gun and stared along its seven-inch barrel at the man on the floor.

Then, without warning, Brewster's left hand appeared from beneath him with one of his own guns in its grip. He somehow managed to squeeze its trigger. A plume of gunsmoke spewed as a deafening bullet ripped across the room and tore past the gunslinger's shoulder.

Fargo gave out a laugh, then pulled back on his own trigger and blasted a deadly reply. The head of Joe Brewster shattered as it took the final bullet.

135

Fargo went to approach when he saw through the window the marshal racing along Main Street towards the hotel.

'Good try, Joey, but you bit off more than you could chew.'

The gunman turned on his heels, ran down the back stairs and trailed the route his fellow hired killers had taken seconds earlier. Fargo reached the three of them and grabbed both bags from Green and Smith before throwing one into the arms of Layne.

'Ben comes with me back to the Texas,' Fargo said quickly as they all reached the lane which ran along the back of all the buildings. He looked at Smith. 'You and Jed go to Doc Hardy's and make sure that that bounty hunter is dead! If he ain't then you kill him!'

Green and Smith did as ordered and hurried down through the shadows towards the back of Hardy's office. With the scent of gunsmoke in their nostrils the gunmen too wanted to get some killing under their belts before the day came to an end.

Monte Bale charged into the lobby of the hotel with his gun at hip level. He was ready for anything. He knew that the shooting had emanated from somewhere inside the hotel. Now he would follow the scent of gunsmoke to its origin.

He climbed the stairs two at a time and reached the landing within seconds. His eyes vainly searched the corridor for danger. Then he saw the smoke drifting from the open door of room three. He strode up to it and looked inside.

With gritted teeth Bale approached the body, then gave out a long angry sigh. It was impossible to tell who lay there with half his face shot off, but he suspected it was Joe Brewster. Bale knew that those he sought had escaped by taking to the back stairs. It was pointless even trying to catch up with them.

As a puffing and panting Doc Hardy reached the landing the marshal rested a shoulder against the corridor wall and holstered his own weapon.

'There's a dead'un in here, Doc.' Bale gestured with his right thumb.

Hardy stopped and tried to get his second wind. 'Who is it?'

'Whoever it is he ain't got a lot of head left on his shoulders,' the marshal warned.

12

A thousand ravenous bats swooped all around the town chasing the moths which were being drawn to the blazing torches outside The Texas House. Lines of men still waited to be fleeced of their meagre savings and neither saw or heard anything of the activity above their heads. All they could think of was being allowed into the palace before them. No Eden could hold greater expectations for the townsfolk. It was as if every eye within the boundaries of the remote oasis town could see only one thing: the splendidly painted doors which, they believed, would lead them to not only paradise but fortune.

The two gunslingers had carried the pair of heavy bags the length of Main Street's back alleyways to remain unseen, and had then crossed the wide dusty thoroughfare, heading towards their goal, the busy gambling hall.

It had been difficult to find enough shadows to shield them from prying eyes but Fargo and Layne had managed it. They carried their hefty burdens down the side of the newly constructed building into the darkness until they reached its guarded door. Gunman Poke Piper was nearly as old as Fargo but had not carved as many notches on his wooden gun grip. He opened the door and ushered the two men inside before closing it.

The wooden stairwell was unlike the rest of the magnificent gambling-hall. This was a private route to Kelly's private offices. Both Fargo and Layne made their way up the narrow flight of steps with the heavy bags in tow. Fargo knocked the door at the top of the dimly illuminated steps and waited.

'It ain't locked!' Kelly's voice rang out.

As they entered the lavishly decorated room they saw Kelly rise from his desk eagerly. The gambler dropped his cigar into the glass tray and met them halfway across the room. He could not conceal his elation.

'This better be worth it, Texas,' Fargo gasped as beads of sweat dripped from his face. 'I almost busted my back carrying these damn bags.'

'What's in them, Texas Jack?' Layne managed to ask.

'A treasure, boys.' Kelly grinned broadly. 'Stolen from a bank by the Brewster brothers and now ours. A golden fortune!'

Layne dropped his bag on the carpet. 'I think I prefer paper money.'

Texas Jack Kelly smiled before snapping his fingers at his men. 'Open them up, Fargo. I want to see what a fortune in gold coin looks like.'

Fargo released his grip on the bag he had carried from the back of the hotel and produced a knife from his pants pocket. He opened its blade, dropped on to one knee and slashed through the canvas.

A few golden coins fell on to the

carpet, then Fargo's expression altered as his eyes and then his hands vainly searched for more.

'What in tarnation?'

Kelly stooped and gazed into the bag. 'What's wrong?'

Fargo did not reply. He turned on his knee and pulled the other bag away from Layne. He stabbed the bag and draped the honed edge of the blade across the canvas until the bag's interior was also exposed. Again a dozen or more golden coins fell from the top of the bag. Fargo dropped his knife and began hauling the contents of both bags on to the carpeted floor.

It was metal but it was nothing like gold coin. Everything from horse shoes to rusted farrier's tools appeared as the pile grew bigger at Fargo's knees.

'We got us a lotta lead and iron here, Texas. But there ain't no more gold that I can find.'

'What?' Kelly screamed out at both men. 'Are you sure these are the right bags? Maybe there were others in the

142

hotel room! Did you look?'

'These are the only two bags there was, Texas.' Fargo looked mystified.

Layne blinked hard as his mind tried to work out what had happened to the fortune he had heard his boss rave about. 'I don't get it, Texas Jack. This is junk. Where's the rest of the golden eagles?'

Kelly straightened up. His eyes narrowed to such an extent that they could not be seen by either of his henchmen. He clenched both fists and paced around the room, staring at the ceiling above them. Then he paused.

'These are the bags from Brewster's room?' he repeated.

'The only bags that were in there, Texas,' Fargo replied. He stood up and patted the rust from his hands.

Kelly glanced at his top gun. 'And Joey?'

'I killed him just like you told me!'

'Damn!' Kelly cursed angrily. 'Joey must have hidden the loot before he reached Desert Springs. He piled this junk in those bags to fool us. Now we can't get him to spill the beans and tell us where he stashed the gold coins.'

Fargo ran a hand across his sweating neck. 'We can't ever find out where he hid it, Texas.'

Texas Jack Kelly turned and looked at Fargo. His left hand rose until he was pointing straight at the confused gunman.

'He came in from the desert,' Kelly muttered like a burning fuse. 'Maybe he hid it out there. Maybe you boys ought to go and try and find it.'

'What?' Layne gulped at the thought of ever going out into the vast desert that fringed the southern part of the town. 'I ain't hankering to ride out there. Not even for a share of a fortune.'

'You will do what I tell you to do, Ben,' Kelly growled angrily. 'I pay you to obey orders and you'll earn your salary any way I say.'

Layne bit his lip. He turned and started to walk back towards the door.

'I quit! You ain't paying me enough to go tangle with no damn desert!'

Texas Jack Kelly pushed past Fargo and stooped. His hand caught hold of the knife. He straightened up and called out at the retreating gunman.

'Hold on up there, Ben!' Kelly said as he continued on to the man with his back to him. 'I got something for you!'

Ben Layne turned just as Kelly reached him. For the first time since the gunman had known the gambler he saw the expression change from its usual expressionless state to one of blind rage. Kelly thrust the knife with all his force into the middle of the stunned Layne. Layne gave out a scream as he felt the sharp blade carve its way into him. His eyes widened and then looked down at the handle of the weapon. Kelly twisted the blade as if he were gutting a fish, then released his grip. Layne coughed blood up and then looked down at the lethal wound.

'Y-you done killed me, Texas Jack!'

Layne said through a mess of gore.

Kelly did not reply as he walked to Fargo's shoulder, then paused. The gambler smiled as Layne dropped on to his knees and clutched at the gore-covered hilt of the knife.

Fargo walked away from his boss and rested his hip on the edge of the desk. He rubbed his whiskers and exhaled. 'You better not try that trick with me, Texas! I'll shoot your eyes out if'n you do!'

Layne fell on to his face. His body twitched as life left it swiftly, leaving only an expanding pool of blood in its wake.

'Nobody quits Texas Jack.' Kelly said, rubbing the blood from his hand down Fargo's vest. 'Not him or you or any of the other vermin I pay. Savvy?'

Fargo looked at the stain on his vest and then back into the face of the man who, he knew, was far more dangerous than his fancy riverboat-style clothing would imply. 'I reckon so, Texas!'

'You and the rest of the boys will

head out into the desert at sunup and see if you can find where Joey hid them gold coins, Fargo,' Kelly announced. He picked up his cigar and placed it between his teeth. He struck another match and touched the ashed tip of his cigar. Smoke billowed around the room.

'Joe might have hidden the gold coins in town after he arrived,' Fargo suggested. 'Maybe we ought to look around the places he went after he got here?'

The gambler sucked in the smoke and closed his eyes as though nothing had happened in his office. He waved a hand. 'You might just be right there, Fargo. But before you do anything get Piper and a few of the other boys to clean up this mess. They can take the carpet out back and burn it!'

'What about Ben here?' The gunfighter eased himself off the desk and rested his hands on the grips of his guns.

'Burn him with it,' Kelly answered bluntly.

The gunman shook his head. 'Oh yeah? I sent Seth and Jed to Hardy's to make sure Iron Eyes is dead.'

Kelly's eyes opened. He looked at Fargo. 'You should have gone yourself, Fargo. I've heard that even half-dead Iron Eyes is more than a match for even the best of gunslingers.'

'You scared of that bounty hunter, Texas?'

'Nope.'

'A man can never tell when you're bluffing.' Fargo looked down at what was left of Layne and then back at the gambler. He licked his dry lips, then gritted his teeth. 'One day you'll play your hand wrong, Texas. Even four aces can be beat.'

Kelly returned to his padded chair and sat down. He changed the subject as his mind returned to the fortune which had so far eluded him.

'I want the rest of them gold coins, Fargo. Savvy?'

'I savvy.' The gunman carefully stepped over the pool of blood which was growing around the lifeless body of Layne. He opened the door to the secret staircase and then looked back at the gambler. 'I'll round up a few of the boys.'

Whatever the gambler was thinking it was well hidden behind the mask of a man who knew how to bluff. Texas Jack Kelly picked up a box of matches from his desk and tossed them the length of the room. Fargo caught them.

'OK?' Kelly asked through a line of cigar smoke.

Fargo swallowed hard. 'Yep.'

13

Jed Green and Seth Smith were not the only people who were headed for the small office belonging to Doc Hardy, although they were the only ones to choose the longer route through the blackness of Main Street's back alleys. Another man with an entirely different agenda had already reached the unimposing wooden structure in answer to the request he had received earlier. The two-room ground-floor office where Hardy had laboured for so long on Iron Eyes was quite dark when the undertaker reached the unlocked front door and entered. With only the desk lamp with its brass wheel turned fully up and the others respectfully adjusted to a dim glow around the table where the body lay beneath a bloodstained white sheet, the office had taken on an eerie atmosphere that even Cyril Perkins noticed. Shadows danced in the flickering amber light on the room's four walls like ill-behaved sprites as the thin figure closed the door behind him.

The light from the glass dome over the desk lamp illuminated the whiskey bottle beside it as the tall, thin man quietly walked towards it. His eyes saw the bottle long before they noticed the table and its draped burden.

Perkins looked every inch the owner of a funeral parlour as he ventured into the silent office. Clad entirely in black and wearing a silk top hat, he moved to the desk and ran a slim finger along the length of the bottle. Perkins was well over six feet in height and nearly as thin as the body which he had come to measure before taking it down to his undertaker's parlour to prepare for the burial. His white sideburns were as wild as his small green eyes. It was said that some folks are created to do certain jobs. Being an undertaker was the only profession that Perkins could ever have done without looking out of place.

Few people ever spoke to Perkins unless they had to do so because he had a way of making people think that he was measuring them up with his eyes for a pine box.

He moved silently, as most of those in his trade did, and paused beside the desk. The thin man who looked little healthier than those he laid to rest placed his knuckles on his hips. He was about to proceed towards the white sheet when his long nose caught the aroma of the expensive whiskey vapours rising from the open neck of the bottle on the desk. Perkins was a man who had consumed most spirits in his time, apart from embalming fluid, although there were many who doubted his vigorous denials concerning even that. His pale complexion looked as though it was he and not those whom he buried who was actually deceased. Temptation was a hard mistress and she had always got the better of Perkins. He plucked the bottle up, held its neck beneath his nose and inhaled deeply.

This was far more inviting than the usual fluids he dealt with and proved impossible to resist to a man who had spent the better part of his fifty years vainly attempting to get the stench of death out of his nose.

'Doc won't miss a couple of fingers,' Perkins muttered. He placed the neck of the bottle to his mouth until the amber liquor started to flow into his mouth. He swallowed and then swallowed again. Then he lowered his arm and gave out a belch. 'Damn! That *is* good stuff!'

Perkins walked with the bottle in his left hand to the table and took another long swig. Satisfied, his thin fingers took the end of the long sheet and pulled it off the nearly naked Iron Eyes. The sheet fell to the floor as the undertaker squinted in the dim light at the unexpected sight before him.

Like a spooked bronco, Perkins reeled in horror at the sight which met his eyes.

'Sweet Lord! Damn it all! What on

earth happened to this poor critter?' Perkins asked himself as he edged closer to the bounty hunter's head. Nervously he bent over to get a better view. 'Reckon this had better be a closed casket job! Nobody will want to set eyes on that face and no mistake!'

After another swig to settle his nerves, Perkins placed the bottle down beside the nearest of the motionless hands and then, in true businesslike manner, he pulled out his tape measure. He unrolled it and put one end at the top of Iron Eyes's head, then he walked the length of the table until he reached the feet. Perkins raised the measure and then looked at the tape. He glanced back at the strange scarred body.

'I don't know who you are but you're the same height as me, son! Exactly the same!' The long-legged undertaker moved around the table and returned on the opposite side of the body. When he reached the torso he measured the chest and noted. 'Pretty wide for a

154

skinny varmint!'

Perkins looked across the room and saw the chair shrouded in shadows. The chair where the bounty hunter's trail coat lay with the pair of matched Navy Colts atop it. The long mule-eared boots stood before the chair and the remnants of Iron Eyes's pants and shirt were next to them. It was obvious to the experienced undertaker that the blood-soaked clothing had been cut from the body and thrown to where they lay before Hardy had started his work.

Perkins licked his lips. They were dry. His green eyes looked across the bounty hunter's chest at the tempting whiskey bottle and its amber contents. He stretched over and grabbed hold of it, then raised it to his mouth and began drinking once again. As he drank he looked at the scars which covered every inch of the body beside him. It seemed impossible that they could be real. Over the years Hardy and Perkins had enjoyed trying to get the better of one another, playing practical jokes which had often risen to ludicrous heights.

With his free hand Perkins started to scratch at the skin of the body. The scars remained intact but he noticed something else. The skin ought to have been cold and yet it felt warm to his fingertips.

Perkins started to nod knowingly. 'I got me a feeling that old Doc is up to one of his childish pranks again!'

Suddenly a strange noise came from the chest of the bounty hunter. It was like a rattler getting ready to strike out at its prey. Startled, Perkins jerked the bottle away from his lips and looked down at Iron Eyes.

Then the noise happened again.

'What the hell was that?' the stunned undertaker asked himself. He prodded the body with straight fingers. 'Get up, boy! you ain't fooling nobody.'

Then the upper part of Iron Eyes's torso jerked with such violence that the chest lifted off the table for a few seconds before returning to where it had rested for over an hour. Perkins's eyes widened in disbelief as they stared down at the chest a mere eighteen inches away from his face. It rose and fell in staggered motion. Even in the dim lamplight he could actually see the heart pounding between the arch of the ribs.

It was beating like a war drum.

'What's going on here?' Perkins gasped and lowered the bottle until it rested on the table next to Iron Eyes's right hand. 'I was told you were dead, boy! Why'd they cover you up under a sheet if you weren't dead? I'm gonna kill Doc for wasting my time like this!'

An amused expression had carved itself into the usually bland features of the owner of the funeral parlour. He went to walk away, then realized that his legs refused to obey. He slapped them hard.

'C'mon! This is just one of old Doc's jokes!' Perkins told his lower limbs. 'I ain't scared, legs! How could I be scared of that? That gotta be the worst make-up I ever seen. Nobody ever looked that bad.'

Perkins placed a hand on the edge of the table to steady himself as he saw the lips of the bounty hunter start to move, as though he were tasting the air for the very first time.

'Where am I?' Iron Eyes croaked. 'Who are you?'

'I knew it! You weren't dead at all! Dead men don't suddenly get undead. Does Doc think he can trick me?' Perkins walked a few inches away from where his feet had felt they were nailed to the floor. He closed his eyes and tried to calm down. He was furious with his old pal. 'This'un will take some bettering, though.'

Iron Eyes's right hand located the whiskey bottle and dragged it up and over his chest until its neck was close to his lips. Perkins watched in stunned terror as the bounty hunter tipped the contents into his mouth and eagerly swallowed the fiery liquid.

'How much did that old fool pay you to play-act like this, boy?' Perkins waved his finger at the bounty hunter. 'Whatever it was he should have saved his money coz you are the most pitiful critter I ever seen. I saw right through you.'

Then a thought occurred to the undertaker.

'Hang on a damn minute here,' he heard himself saying as he stared at Iron Eyes. 'I got me a feeling that old Doc might be hiding around here watching.'

The bounty hunter paused his drinking and looked through blurred eyes at the smiling man beside the table. 'Are you the sawbones, mister?'

'No I ain't!' Perkins snapped back. 'I'm the undertaker.'

'But I ain't dead,' Iron Eyes said.

'We both knows that, boy.'

A sense of relief washed over the undertaker. He felt himself calming down fast as he leaned against the table with his back to Iron Eyes.

'Get on up, boy.' Perkins laughed out loud. 'The joke's on you and old Doc. I seen through you. Ha! I should have known that nobody could look as bad as you.'

The sound of the back door in the rear room opening suddenly filled Perkins's ears. He smiled as best his withered face could actually smile.

'Who's that?' Iron Eyes released the bottle.

'You know full well who that is.' The undertaker frowned. 'I hear you back there, Doc. It didn't work, you old fool. Come on in here. Your pal here couldn't hold his breath long enough to fool me.'

The sound of two pairs of boots rang through the structure as Texas Jack's men walked out of the shadows into the light. Seth Smith and Jed Green entered the office with their guns drawn and levelled. They watched as the undertaker's expression changed once again. This time it went from amusement to confusion.

'Who are they?' Iron Eyes whispered.

'Damned if I know, boy.' Perkins took

a step towards the gunmen between the table and the doorway. 'You ain't old Doc Hardy. Who in the name of the Lord are you and what you doing here?'

'Where's Iron Eyes?' Green asked.

'He's on that table there, Jed.' Smith pointed with his free hand. 'See him?'

'I see him.'

'He ain't dead.'

'He will be.'

Again Perkins closed the distance between them. 'Put those guns away, boys. This joke's gone far enough. Ain't nobody laughing any more. Where's old Doc?'

Without warning both gunmen fanned their hammers in answer to Perkins's innocent question. They gleefully watched as the undertaker was lifted off his feet by the bullets which hit his chest dead centre. Both fired again, sending their lead after the body before it crashed into the wall. The office echoed to the sound of the deafening noise.

Acrid gunsmoke filled the distance

between the table and the hot barrels of their. 45s.

'Now we finish the famous Iron Eyes off. C'mon!' Seth Smith snarled as he walked forward through the choking gunsmoke with Green at his side. Their thumbs clawed back on their hammers until their weapons fully locked.

Neither man squeezed his trigger, though.

It was Green who stopped first.

Then Smith became rooted to the spot.

They waved the dense, lingering gunsmoke away with their free hands and stared at the long, empty table. Green spun full circle on his heels as his eyes vainly searched the dimly lit room in desperation.

Jed Green stared at the table and its dried-gore covered surface.

Only the whiskey bottle remained upon it.

A cold shiver raced up Green's spine as he stared at the table. 'He was there. Buck naked, Seth! I seen him there.

Iron Eyes was lying there buck naked.'

'I know that. I seen him as well.'

'Men can't disappear into thin air, can they?'

'W-where'd he go then?' Smith stammered.

A whistle attracted their attention. 'You looking for me?'

The gunmen swung round to where the trail coat lay on the chair, but the pair of Navy Colts were no longer upon its bloodstained fabric.

They fired again frantically at the dancing shadows upon the wall. The coat rose into the air as their bullets tore it to shreds. Both men continued firing until their guns were empty.

'Did we get him?' Smith asked as he feverishly reloaded.

'How the hell do I know?' Green responded as his fingers clawed at fresh bullets from his gunbelt. 'I can't see nothing except our smoke.'

Then in the shadows they heard a sound coming from just beyond the table. It was the unmistakable sound of laughter. Iron Eyes staggered out into the dim lamplight with both his guns in his hands.

'Oh my God! Look at him!' Smith yelped like a dog with its tail caught in a trap. The faster he tried to get bullets into his smoking chambers the more of them fell to the floor.

'That ain't no real man,' Green gulped.

Iron Eyes paused and inhaled deeply.

'Who sent you to kill me?' he asked.

Both men stared at the horrific sight before them. Neither had ever witnessed anything which came close to describing how the bounty hunter appeared.

They dropped their guns and raised their arms.

'Answer me,' the bounty hunter snarled.

'Texas Jack Kelly,' Green blurted out.

Iron Eyes took a deep breath and looked straight at Smith. 'Is that right? Is your pard telling me the truth?'

Smith nodded. 'Sure is, Iron Eyes.'

'Who is this Texas Jack varmint?'

'He's the owner of The Texas House! He sent us here to kill you!'

Iron Eyes stepped even closer. 'Why?'

'On account of him being wanted and you being a bounty hunter and all,' Green blurted. 'He figured it was best if you were dead!'

Smith blinked hard as the gunsmoke burned into his eyes. 'Can we go now?'

'Yeah! You can go.' A twisted smile crept across Iron Eyes's face. He cocked his hammers and then mercilessly pulled on both his triggers. White plumes of lethal ear-busting vengeance spewed from the barrels of the bounty hunter's weapons. The two men flew backward and landed in the blackness of the rear room. 'To Hell!'

14

Nothing could have alerted them to the horrors that they would discover inside the doctor's small home when the trio of oddly assorted men responded to the sound of the gunfire. They had been close to the newly opened Texas House when the distant crackle of gunplay rang out along the length and breadth of Main Street. They had been heading from the hotel to the lane beside Cooper's store to see if the body Joshua had discovered was still there. All that changed when the shooting started. With Doc Hardy and his deputy in tow, Marshal Bale made his way back towards the place from where he was sure the gunfire had come. They had been 200 yards away from the small wooden building when the last of the shots were fired. The flashing of lead lightning had lit up the front window and drawn the keen-eyed Bale towards it. Yet when they had arrived all that greeted them were three freshly dispatched corpses and the smell of gunpowder.

Doc Hardy stood in the centre of the bloody floor as Marshal Bale turned each of the lamps up until their light filled the office. The deputy had not moved from the doorframe and simply stood open-mouthed, staring in disbelief at the horrific sight which had greeted them all when they answered the call of the round of gunshots they had heard only minutes earlier.

Hardy was in a state of shock. He could not comprehend the carnage which had occurred inside the building he had lived and worked in for so many years. His wrinkled eyes darted from one body to the next and then repeated the futile action. Then he saw the blood-splattered walls and the bullet holes in the plaster and woodwork. He had tended those who had found themselves on the wrong side of a shooting-iron more times than he could recall, but it was the first time anything like this had occurred within the sanctity of his own home. It chilled him to the bone.

As Bale moved back to him the old medical man gripped the lawman's arm in a way he had never done before. Hardy was shaking as the enormity of the situation washed over him like floodwater.

Bale looked into the old eyes, then guided Hardy to the desk chair and sat him down.

'Easy, Doc. I know this must be a shock to you, seeing your office all shot up like this. We'll sort it out for you.'

Hardy rubbed his face. 'What in tarnation went on in here, Monte? I don't cotton this at all.'

Joshua ventured across the floor nervously. He glanced at the two dead gunslingers lying in the rear room where the force of Iron Eyes's bullets had propelled them. He cleared his throat and then rested beside the desk.

'Glory be,' Joshua managed to say. 'This is just awful. It's a good thing you was out with us and not in here when the bullets started flying. You'd be as dead as these critters and no mistake. Yep, Doc! You'd be lying there in a pool of blood just like they are.'

'Shut up!' Bale clipped the back of his deputy's head as he walked from the desk to where the undertaker lay crumpled on the floor. He frowned at the body of Cyril Perkins and raised his eyebrows before pointing.

'Somebody stole Perkins's pants,' he said drily. 'And his long tail coat as well!'

Both his companions looked at the body of the undertaker and then returned their gaze to the tall marshal.

'Who'd steal old Cyril's pants and coat, Monte?' the deputy asked. 'I mean, the critter was like a beanpole. Who'd fit into his cast-offs anyways?'

Suddenly Hardy stood and stared straight at the long table in the middle of the room. 'And who the hell would go and steal Iron Eyes?'

The marshal went to the table and rested both hands upon it as he tried to work out an answer which made some sense. Suddenly he noticed that the Navy Colts and mule-eared boots were also missing. He glanced back at the seated Hardy.

'Didn't I see Iron Eyes's guns and boots over by that chair earlier, Doc?' he enquired. 'They seem to have disappeared.'

Hardy looked at the bullet-scarred chair and nodded. 'Yep. They was there but they're sure gone now.'

Bale turned. 'If I didn't know any better I'd say that it was Iron Eyes himself that killed those gunmen in your back room, Doc.'

Joshua gave a half-smile. 'That ain't possible, Monte. Doc said he was dead. Ain't that right, Doc? Iron Eyes was dead.'

'But his guns and boots are gone, Joshua,' Bale pointed out with a long hard look at the bullet-riddled chair. 'Who else but Iron Eyes would take them? Who else would even want them?'

Joshua nodded and shook his head in turn as one thought replaced another in his young mind. 'But his clothes are still there! He couldn't go anywheres naked! I know folks around here are pretty casual about most things but I reckon they'd notice a long, tall, naked fella pretty darn fast.'

Bale smiled then looked back at Perkins's body. 'And old Cyril has no pants or coat on! Do you reckon that he and our bounty-hunting friend are about the same size? I do.'

Hardy rubbed his whiskers even harder. 'This is madness. It can't be.'

'Have you another explanation, Doc?' Bale asked. 'I can see someone killing for money or even to steal guns but why would anyone steal a body? Crazy as it seems, I think Iron Eyes is somehow still alive.'

'But he was dead,' the deputy

insisted. 'Doc told us.'

'Wait up a minute.' Hardy's expression slowly changed. His mind began to wrestle with the lifetime of knowledge he had gathered and all the knowledge from countless books that he had absorbed over the previous decades. He rose slowly to his feet, ambled to the side of the marshal and his underling. 'You know something, Monte?'

'What?'

'I recall reading about a number of cases years back about folks who were buried alive because folks thought they were dead,' Hardy said. 'When they opened up their coffins they found scratch marks on the underside of the coffin lids where the poor critters had desperately tried to get out!'

Joshua winced. 'Buried alive?'

Hardy nodded. 'Yep! Buried alive! You see, there is a rare medical condition which makes a subject appear to be dead. No detectable pulse or heartbeat and the like but in fact the patient is actually in some kind of deep coma.'

Bale looked at Hardy. 'Could Iron Eyes have been in this sort of coma, Doc?'

The doctor shrugged. 'I can't say for certain but it sure looks like it. That gentleman has defied medical science for most of his life judging by all the scars he's carrying. If anyone could have gone into that sort of deep sleep, it's him.'

Joshua looked sickly. 'That means that when I die and they bury me I might be still alive. I sure don't like the sound of that!'

Marshal Bale clipped the back of his deputy's head again to draw his attention. 'Don't go fretting none, Joshua. I'll make sure that when you're dead they bury you shallow and put a bugle in the box with you!'

Doc Hardy then looked at his desk again. He saw that the plate with its napkin had been removed. 'Hell! My steak supper's gone, Monte!'

Then Joshua grabbed hold of both of his friends and turned them towards the bullet riddled chair where what was left of the bounty hunter's trail coat lay in mutilated ribbons.

'Look!' Joshua pointed.

Both men looked.

'What we looking at, boy?' Hardy asked.

'I see it!' Monte Bale began to smile and then took a step closer to the chair and crouched down. His trigger finger pointed at the floor and the unmistakable bloody footprints. 'This is where a man with bare feet put on his boots!'

Joshua bent double and found more footprints marked in blood on the floor. 'Well, glory be! It must be Iron Eyes! He ain't dead at all!'

'You know what that means, boys?' Hardy clapped his hands together and for the briefest of moments he looked like someone in prayer.

'Yep!' Bale stood up to his full height and grinned at the doctor. 'It means that you saved Iron Eyes's life!'

Hardy nodded firmly. 'Damn right I did!'

'It's just a shame that he went on a killing spree and slaughtered all these folks though.' The deputy sighed. 'Maybe being in that coma unhinged him a tad.'

'Iron Eyes didn't kill Perkins, Joshua.' Bale corrected the younger lawman.

'Are you sure?'

Bale pointed at the undertaker's body. 'Old Cyril was hit by .45s! Those two gunmen back there have .45s! They killed Perkins, not our bounty-hunting friend!'

'And Iron Eyes killed them varmints by the look of them holes in their chests,' Hardy added knowingly. 'Navy Colts are only .36s! Look at the size of the holes in their chests. Small and deadly the way a Navy Colt kills. Yep, he finished them off after they killed old Cyril.'

'That was sure neighbourly of him.' Joshua frowned.

The marshal looked from one room

to the next. 'Doc's dead right. The way I see it is that old Cyril came here in answer to the message Joshua delivered and then those two varmints showed up. They killed Cyril and somehow Iron Eyes recovered fast enough to kill them.'

'Why'd they come here for anyways?' the deputy asked scratching his head.

'To kill the bounty hunter,' Bale answered. 'What other reason would they have?'

'And a bounty hunter is only feared by someone with a price on his head,' Hardy muttered. 'Someone was mighty scared that Iron Eyes would recover and then realize that there was a bounty just waiting to be had.'

Joshua walked to the two dead bodies laid out in the back room and tapped his teeth thoughtfully. 'You know something? I seen these critters before, Monte.'

'And me, Joshua. They work for Texas Jack,' Monte Bale said as he strode out of the office. 'C'mon!'

'Where we going, Monte?' Joshua

called out, trying to keep pace with the
marshal.

'To pay a visit to Texas Jack before
Iron Eyes gets to him first,' came the
reply.

15

It is said that there is nothing more dangerous than a wounded animal. The same was true of Iron Eyes. For when he was in pain he became even more lethal. There was an eerie silence across the outskirts of the oasis town as the strangely dressed figure lurched his way toward his goal. Nothing dared make a sound, for the hunter was at large. The hunter of both animal and men alike was on the move. Confused and racked with pain Iron Eyes still knew what he had to do. He had to reach his horse and the saddlebags containing his ammunition. There was only one place where his magnificent stallion could be and that was the town's livery stable.

The clothes he had taken from the undertaker's body fitted well and there was just enough slack in the waistband to hold his trusty Navy Colts against his skin. Since leaving Doc Hardy's place he had followed his nose to the livery stable set at the furthermost end of Desert Springs. All stables had an aroma that even blind folks could sense.

Like a wounded animal he had used every shadow there was to avoid being seen by anyone. Iron Eyes had travelled surprisingly quickly for a man who had, only an hour earlier, been measured for a pine box. It was as if death itself had suited the corpselike figure. Refreshed him in some perverse way.

The bounty hunter knelt in the bushes beside a stream and stared at the tall building where he knew he would find his palomino stallion. He cupped his hands, brought the ice-cold water to his face and washed the grime from his eyes.

Then he dropped his hand into the unfamiliar coat pocket and pulled what was left of the steak he had stolen from Doc Hardy's supper plate. His sharp teeth gnawed at the cold meat like a hound with a bone. He chewed and chewed until only gravy remained on his fingers. He sucked at the gravy until his hand was clean.

Iron Eyes continued to stare at the tall building as though in a trance. He pulled the bottle of whiskey from the opposite pocket and drank until the taste of the food was washed from his mouth. Then he slowly rose to his full height. Suddenly he heard the horses inside the stable whinnying.

He was upwind and they could smell his scent.

After returning the bottle to his pocket he ran his bony fingers through his mane of sweat-soaked hair until his face could feel the gentle night breeze on his skin. He was befuddled at what must have happened to him. All he could recall was talking to the marshal; and then there was nothing until he woke up and saw Cyril Perkins looming over him with a tape measure in his hands.

Then Iron Eyes remembered the gunslingers. Their loud voices and even louder guns when they opened up. What had happened after that was still clouded in a mixture of nightmare and reality to the bounty hunter. He did recall killing them though.

But was that really what had happened? Was it? Or was it just part of the mysterious place he had found himself travelling through as he battled with nightmares.

Then he looked down at his belly and the guns he had rammed into his pants belt. The barrels of his guns were still warm against his belly.

It had been real.

His memory began slowly to return. Not all at once but in teasing little wisps. He knew that he had killed them because they had tried to kill him. They had also just killed the man whose clothes he now wore. That was real.

Iron Eyes knew that now he had to find the man who had paid them. The man they said was wanted dead or alive.

Texas Jack Kelly. That was the name which kept returning to his thoughts.

The name of the man the two misfits had claimed had ordered them to do his dirty work.

Iron Eyes stared at the livery stable. A solitary lantern could be seen inside the building. The tall man listened to the terrified horses. His mind kept chanting the name of Texas Jack Kelly. The gunslingers had said that he was wanted but the bounty hunter could not remember ever hearing of him. He leaned down and pulled the Bowie knife free of his boot neck and stared at its blade.

His eyes then returned to the livery and he began to walk towards it. The closer he got the louder the horses became. They could always smell him, he thought. Horses could smell the aroma of death no matter how hard he tried to rid himself of its acrid aroma. Even the new clothes could not hide the scent of a man who had lived alongside death for so many years.

As he reached the wide-open double-doors of the loosely constructed building he heard the angry voice of a man obviously woken from a deep sleep.

Iron Eyes paused and clutched the knife in his hand. He heard the man telling the horses to calm down but they were far too smart to listen to him. He was just a blacksmith and unable to sense the danger which loomed in the darkness beyond the doors.

'Hush the hell up!' the man said for the umpteenth time as he walked along the line of stalls and tried to pacify the nervous animals. 'Quiet! I was having me a real nice dream and you critters spoiled it. Hush now! You hear me?'

The man reached for his lantern and turned its wheel. The vast interior of the stables lit up. Then to his horror he saw the ghostlike figure in the doorway.

'Who are you?' he asked, fearfully edging backwards to where he kept his scattergun. 'Speak up! If you got a name, spill it!'

'Iron Eyes,' the bounty hunter said in a rasping whisper.

'Is that a name?' The man continued

backing until his groping fingers located the double-barrelled weapon propped up against the wall. 'You stay where you are now!'

Iron Eyes walked into the livery and looked around until he saw his palomino in a stall at the end of the long line of stalls. He could see his saddle and bags perched on the wooden partition beside it. He kept on walking towards it.

'Where you going?' The man picked up the scattergun as quietly as he could and pulled back on its large hammers.

'I've come for my horse.' Iron Eyes reached the tall stallion and looked into its eyes. It was the only horse in the building that was not making a sound. 'And my bags.'

The man started to walk after the tall figure. 'Why you dressed like that? You an undertaker?'

'Nope, but the man who owned these clothes was.' Iron Eyes turned and stared at the ostler. The man stopped in his tracks when he saw the face which was looking straight back at him.

'Holy smoke!' The man started to shake. He brought the massive gun up and trained it on the bounty hunter. 'Who did you say you was?'

'Iron Eyes.'

The man swallowed hard. 'I heard that name earlier. They said you was dead over at Doc Hardy's.'

'I was.'

'Git out of here.'

'I'd drop that cannon if I was you,' Iron Eyes said in a low, threatening tone.

The ostler saw the knife in the bony hand. A bead of sweat ran down his face.

'Now why would I want to do that?'

'Because I'll kill you if you don't.' Iron Eyes looked at the stallion. From the corner of his eye he could see the scattergun being lowered. 'You got brains.'

16

When some men wear a marshal's tin star it takes on the aura of a medieval warrior's shield. For courage can never be measured in the same way that men measure other things by. Courage is invisible and it is only its champions and their selfless bravado that makes evil men shy away back into the slime from which they crawled. With torchlight bathing over him and his deputy, Marshal Bale rested his knuckles on the grips of his holstered guns and squared up to the two guards outside The Texas House.

'Get out of my way!' Bale demanded.

'And why should we do that, Marshal?' the nearest guard asked in a low sneer.

'Because if you don't your boss might up and find himself dead,' the marshal growled. 'You understand?'

'What?' the other guard chipped in.

'There's a varmint coming to get Texas Jack!' Joshua added over the shoulder of the marshal.

'Texas Jack ain't scared of nobody,' one of the heavily armed men informed the deputy.

'He oughta be real scared because Iron Eyes just killed two of your worthless gun-packers.' Bale smiled. 'Now we reckon he's coming to kill the varmint who sent them to their deaths!'

The information hit both men hard. One guard looked to the other and then they parted as sweetly as the Red Sea when confronted by Moses. Bale led Joshua into the gambling-hall, then paused as a handsome female no more than sixteen years old moved towards them with a tray bearing fluted glasses filled with sparkling wine.

'You boys want a drink?' she asked them. 'It's free!'

Joshua reached out, then felt the palm of Bale's left hand catch him behind the ear. He winced and saw the broad-shouldered marshal lean close to the sweet-smelling female and whisper something into her ear. Her face suddenly lost the smile and she pointed up the stairs. Bale touched the brim of his hat, then glanced at his deputy before marching towards the carpeted flight of steps. 'C' mon!'

The pair of lawmen climbed the staircase to the landing and looked around. Bale aimed a finger down the long corridor to the door with 'private' painted upon it.

'Is that his office, Monte?' Joshua straightened his gunbelt and blinked nervously.

Bale did not say a word. He just started for the door with a stride few men could have matched for length or purpose. The deputy was almost running just to keep up with his superior.

The marshal grabbed hold of the gleaming doorhandle and turned it hard. He entered the room fast and unexpectedly.

'Kelly!' Bale boomed at the man

behind the desk.

Texas Jack jumped up from his chair in surprise. His eyes strayed from the intruders and darted to the large area in the room from where the blood-soaked carpet and the body had only just been removed. He then returned his attention to the man with the marshal's star pinned to his chest. He tried to look calm but for once his poker face let him down. Sweat trailed down from his neatly combed hair as he walked round his desk with his hand held out.

'Marshal Bale,' Kelly greeted in a faltering tone. 'I'm pleased that you have decided to honour me with a visit on this our opening night of business.'

Bale did not shake the hand.

'You just lost two of your boys, Texas Jack.'

The gambler's hand fell to his side as the words sank in. He turned away from the pair of uninvited guests and made his way to a cabinet where numerous bottles and glasses stood. He poured himself a whiskey and then downed it. His head tilted and his eyes stared at the large lawman.

'How could that be, Bale?' Kelly bluffed. 'All my boys are here. Some downstairs and some around the building. I don't have anyone missing.'

'Is that so?' Bale smiled and strode to where the man was pouring himself another large measure of the fiery liquor. He watched Kelly swallow it.

'Yep! That's so.' Kelly could hear the nervous sound of his own voice as he paced to the back window and stared down into the yard where the blazing bonfire was already consuming the body of Ben Layne and the expensive chunk of carpet it was wrapped in. 'All my employees are here!'

'Except the two lying dead in Doc Hardy's office, Kelly.'

The gambler swung around. His expression betrayed him. 'I don't understand, Marshal.'

'I know those boys worked for you,' Bale shouted.

'They might have but I probably fired

them.' Kelly shrugged. 'Can you prove otherwise?'

Bale raised a finger and then noticed the bare spot on the otherwise well-carpeted floor. He paced across the room and then looked down at the bare boards. Without looking at the gambler he asked a pointed question.

'You like fresh meat, Texas Jack?'

'What?' Kelly edged to his desk and rested both hands down on its polished surface.

Bale looked at the man and then pointed down. 'I was just wondering if you liked fresh meat coz it looks like you bin doing some butchering right here!'

Kelly cleared his throat. 'Get out!'

Joshua walked to where the marshal was aiming his trigger finger and then knelt. He ran his own fingers in the gaps between the floorboards and looked at their tips.

'This is blood, Monte.'

'I figured that, Joshua.'

'Get out!' the gambler shouted.

Bale turned to face Kelly and stood squarely as his hand hovered above his gun grip. He kept on smiling. It was a smile that had unnerved more men than he could number.

'Who died here, Texas Jack?' Bale asked.

'Nobody died no place.' Kelly snorted as his mind raced. 'I got me the best lawyer in Desert Springs and he'll have your job for this outrage. Besides, what has a spot of blood, if it is blood, got to do with two men being killed at the other end of Main Street? Like I said, my lawyer will have your job before sunup!'

Bale shook his head. 'He'll not want my job, Texas Jack. The pay ain't good enough. Now raise them hands.'

Joshua stood back up and rubbed the blood down the side of his britches. He stared at the face of the gambler and raised both eyebrows. 'You look mighty scared there, Mr Kelly!'

'Am I under arrest?' Kelly walked away from the desk and towards the secret utility door. Each step was slow and deliberate.

'I heard you were wanted somewhere!' Bale said. 'Reckon if I lock you up for a few days we might find out whether it's true or not! I have a mountain of Wanted posters in my desk to check!'

Kelly gritted his teeth. 'This is ridiculous, Marshal! I'm not wanted anywhere for anything.'

'We'll see.'

'Two gunmen get shot in the doctor's office and you come after me?' Kelly rested beside the door, His eyes burned across at the marshal. If looks could kill the lawmen would have been already dead. 'Now you claim that I'm a wanted man! This is total garbage, Marshal. I'm a respectable businessman and you seem to be a little jealous.'

'Didn't you have a couple of partners when you arrived in Desert Springs?' Bale smiled. 'They're dead as well, as I recall.'

'Accidents,' Kelly snapped angrily.

'I told you to raise them hands!' Bale repeated his demand.

Kelly forced a smile of his own. 'Perhaps you want a slice of the profits? I've heard that other lawmen get a percentage of businesses to supplement their pitiful salaries! Is that it? Do you want that I go to my desk and open my petty cash box? Is that what this is all about?'

Bale inhaled deeply. 'I actually came here to save your life, Texas Jack. Once you're in one of my cells in the jailhouse you'll be safe. Safe until we find that Wanted poster, that is.'

'Safe from what?' Kelly asked.

'Iron Eyes is gunning for you,' the marshal said.

'Iron Eyes?' Kelly looked away. 'I've not heard of him.'

'Then why did you send them gunslingers to kill him?' Joshua asked.

Suddenly without warning the door beside the gambler opened and Poke Piper came through it clumsily. He stopped in his tracks when he saw the two lawmen standing less than ten feet away.

Faster than either starpacker had imagined possible, Kelly grabbed hold of the burly gunman and hauled his guns from their holsters. He raised his right leg and kicked Piper into the arms of Bale. Kelly blasted a bullet from each gun as he backed into the dark stairwell. As the marshal fell beneath the hefty Piper, the stunned deputy went for his gun. His fingers had only just located the grip when the gambler fired again.

As Monte Bale hit the floor under the weight of the gunman he saw Joshua plucked off his feet as the bullet tore into him.

Then the door slammed shut behind the gambler.

Mustering all his strength Bale pushed the gunman off him and rolled over on to his knees beside his deputy. His eyes found the torn shoulder quickly.

'Glory be, Monte! He done shot me!'

Bale got up and started to tear at the locked door, 'It's just a flesh wound. Get yourself over to Doc's.'

Joshua clambered off the floor, clutching his shoulder with his hand. Blood trickled through his fingers.

'Where you going?'

At last the door gave way and Bale tore it off its hinges. The marshal dragged his Colt from its holster and cocked its hammer. His eyes narrowed as he squinted down the dark steps.

'I'm gonna catch me a fox and teach him it don't pay to shoot my deputy!'

As Bale disappeared into the darkness, Joshua staggered to the office door as more of Kelly's guards arrived in the corridor. The deputy pushed his way between them, then raised his voice.

'Out the way! Wounded lawman coming on through here! Hey, I reckon you boys better go and find yourselves some new kind of employment. If Texas Jack don't outrun Marshal Bale he'll more than likely find himself deader than my Aunt Bessie!'

* * *

Kelly had been running until his legs gave out. He fell and crawled under a fence and lay amid the long grass beneath a tall tree with branches which stretched out twenty feet in all directions. For a few heartbeats the blackness made him feel safe. The gambler rapidly checked the guns he still clung on to. There were enough bullets in their chambers, he silently told himself. He raised himself up and rested his back against the fence posts. Kelly knew that he had put good distance between himself and the marshal he was fleeing from.

Ten years and his sordid past had finally returned to destroy him. He remembered the days when he had travelled on the riverboats and learned his profession from the best gamblers on the Mississippi. It seemed like only yesterday to the exhausted man.

He cursed the fact that he had never been satisfied with simply cheating at the poker tables. For he had a dark side which always wanted more and more. It had never been enough to simply take a rich man's fortune from him. He had to destroy the man as well. If that meant killing him, Texas Jack had obliged.

Maybe it was the fact that on the great river it was easy to get away with killing a man and to dispose of the body in waters which were as wide as some seas. It had become like a drug to the gambler. The risk of getting caught lured him on like a temptress whom he was unable to resist. It had become even more exciting than playing in a poker game with five useless cards but a mountain of skill at bluffing.

Kelly got to his feet and looked over the fence. There was no sign of Bale or anyone else. He rested and tried to get his second wind as he remembered the time when he left the riverboats but continued to kill those who got in his way.

Ten years ago Kelly had been caught and sentenced to be hanged but Lady

Luck had smiled upon him and he had escaped. Again he looked over the fence. He was wanted dead or alive and he knew that it was only a matter of time before Bale or Iron Eyes found a copy of that ancient Wanted poster. He was only worth $1,000. He laughed. He had lost more than that in a single hand of five-card stud.

A thought occurred to Kelly. A chilling thought. Now his hired men would turn on him. For their loyalty was purchased with money and now he only had the wealth within his pockets. A few coins and a billfold with less than $500 were all there was and the gambler knew it might not be enough.

Suddenly he heard a sound to his right. Someone was coming towards him through the dense brush. Kelly swung around, threw himself forward and squeezed both triggers. The deafening sound rang out as the blasts from his gun barrels spewed their venom. He heard a man cry out in pain and knew that he had hit his target.

As he lay in the grass he heard the choking of the man he had just shot getting louder.

'Got you!' Kelly heard himself say victoriously.

He scrambled back to his feet and gripped his guns firmly. He was ready to fire them again when he saw the figure staggering out into the starlight.

Kelly's face went ashen.

It was Fargo.

'Fargo?' Kelly raced to the man as he fell at his feet.

'I-I come to tell you . . . ' Fargo coughed and then his head rolled to one side and blood poured from the corner of his mouth.

Kelly knelt and shook the gunfighter. 'Tell me what? Tell me what? Fargo! What were you gonna say?'

It was no good. No amount of shaking would alter the simple truth. Fargo was dead. Whatever he was going to tell the gambler would never be uttered. It was going with him to the bowels of Hell.

Texas Jack Kelly got to his feet and looked all around him. A fear like nothing he had ever felt before swept over him. He looked in all directions, then leaned over and unbuckled Fargo's gunbelt. He looped it around his own waist and checked the holstered guns. They were better than those he had taken from Poke Piper. These were well-balanced, gunfighter's weapons. He tossed the other guns aside and flicked off the small safety loops from their hammers.

'I have to get me a horse!' Kelly told himself. 'A damn good horse!'

The tired gambler pushed his way through a wall of high weeds and then his eyes lit up. There outside the livery stables stood a handsome and powerful palomino stallion. It was already saddled and just waiting for him. It was as if his prayers had been answered.

'That's my ticket out of here,' Kelly told himself as he started toward the animal. 'There ain't another horse in this town that could catch that critter.

Lady Luck is still my sweetheart!'

Defying his own weariness he reached the horse within seconds and ran his hand along its neck. This was the finest horseflesh he had ever seen, he told himself.

Kelly took hold of the reins and went to raise his left leg when a man shuffled out into the starlight from the livery stable. The ruthless gambler drew one of the Peacemakers, cocked its hammer and fired. The man spun like a top and crashed into the ground. Kelly laughed and led the horse to the body and kicked it over. He stared down at the ostler as smoke trailed from the barrel of the gun.

'Reckon you must be the owner of this fine animal,' Kelly said to the body as he pushed a boot into the stirrup and hauled himself on top of the stallion. 'Tell the folks in heaven that Texas Jack Kelly just took your nag!'

As the gambler was about to holster the smoking Peacemaker he heard the sound of footsteps come from behind him. He swung the mighty stallion around and saw the man in black walking towards him. It was a sight straight from the depths of his worst nightmare.

The voice was more akin to a whisper. 'That's my horse, Texas Jack,' Iron Eyes hissed as he aimed both his Navy Colts at the man astride his horse.

Kelly cocked his hammer. 'Who the hell are you?'

'I'm the man who's gonna kill you,' the bounty hunter said as he stepped even closer. 'I'm Iron Eyes!'

The name resounded in the gambler's mind. Kelly held the palomino in check and trained his gun straight at the horrific figure. The bounty hunter did not appear to have an ounce of fear in his thin body. He stood firm and raised both his Navy Colts until they were at hip height.

Before the gambler could squeeze the trigger of the Peacemaker Iron Eyes unleashed the fury of his own weaponry.

Two white-hot rods of roaring lightning cut through the darkness between them. The bullets found their target and ripped into the centre of the gambler. Kelly was lifted off the back of the stallion's saddle by the sheer force of the impact. He was thrown through the air like a rag doll and crashed into the wall of the livery.

A trail of blood marked the side of the wooden building as the gambler slid to the ground. He lay in a crumpled heap with the gun still hanging on his lifeless, curled trigger finger.

The bounty hunter forced his guns back into his belt, walked to the stallion and took its reins in his bony left hand. He mounted in one well-practised action and nodded to himself. He gathered the reins, looked down at the dead gambler and spat his contempt.

'You should have stuck to playing poker, Texas Jack!' Iron Eyes drawled, plucking the whiskey bottle from his coat pocket and finishing its fiery contents. 'You ain't worth a damn with a six-shooter!'

He tossed the empty bottle away and was about to head on back into the heart of Desert Springs when he saw the unmistakable figure of Marshal Bale running towards him.

Monte Bale reached the neck of the stallion, paused and glanced at the two dead men before looking up into the face of the bounty hunter.

'You kill them?' Bale asked.

A twisted smile etched the side of Iron Eyes's face. 'He killed the liveryman! I killed him!'

Bale holstered his gun and rubbed his neck. 'We'll have to find out how much Kelly's worth, Iron Eyes!'

'One thousand dollars dead or alive, Marshal,' the bounty hunter told him as he tapped his spurs against the sides of the palomino and began to steer it back towards the town. 'I just remembered!'

The marshal looked at the strange rider and then back down at what was left of Texas Jack Kelly. Two deadly accurate bullet holes had pierced the middle of his shirt.

'Was it a fair fight, Iron Eyes?'

'As fair as it can ever be, friend,' Iron Eyes replied over his broad shoulder.

'What you mean?' Bale pressed.

Their eyes met across the distance. 'He should have known that you can't kill a dead man, Marshal,' Iron Eyes said, and then tapped his spurs harder.

The lawman sighed deeply and watched the horseman disappear into the blackness like a phantom. He suddenly felt cold. Real cold.

Finale

Marshal Monte Bale had not had a wink of sleep and as the blazing sun rose into the heavens above Desert Springs he felt that if he dared to close his eyes he would not awaken for a week. He had just come from Doc Hardy's office with his wounded but jolly deputy. Joshua Peck seemed to want everyone along Main Street to see and know why he had his arm in a sling. The marshal reached their office and sat down on one of the pair of hardback chairs on its boardwalk. He pulled the brim of his Stetson down over his eyes as the younger man chatted to all who tried to go about their morning rituals.

'Will you shut up any time soon, Joshua?' Bale asked.

'OK, Monte!' The deputy ought to have been offended but he was too excited about the previous night's exertions. He sat down beside the older man and continued to nod to everyone with a smile as wide as the street itself. 'I'll shut up if you buy me some breakfast.'

Bale looked from beneath his hat brim. 'You just ate half of Doc's breakfast, boy.'

Joshua touched his arm. 'I lost me a heap of blood last night and I gotta make it up. I sure am powerful hungry.'

Bale pushed his hat back on to his head and sat upright when he caught the aroma of fresh-brewed coffee coming from inside their office. Both men stood and looked at the door. It was unlocked. Curiously the tired lawman pushed the door inward and then saw the tall figure dressed in the undertaker's clothes pouring himself a cup of coffee from their blackened pot.

Iron Eyes glanced up. 'Marshal!'

'What you doing here?' Bale asked.

'I busted in here last night to use one of your cots,' The bounty hunter downed the black beverage, placed the cup down and then stepped out into the hot sunlight. His eyes narrowed as he stared across at the stagecoach depot with an intensity which made both lawmen curious.

'Why?'

Iron Eyes pointed at the stagecoach depot. 'I seen a *hombre* go into that office when I reached here last night, Marshal. I reckoned that he might be worth keeping an eye on. He had himself a mighty heavy bag in tow!'

Both Bale and Joshua looked to the building where the bounty hunter was staring like an eagle ready to swoop down on its unsuspecting prey. Then the door of the depot waiting-room opened and a small, well-dressed man emerged with a bag that barely cleared the floor.

'Why, that's Rufe from the hotel!' Joshua said.

Bale raised an eyebrow when he saw the effort it cost the small man to carry his bag. Rufe Carter had to place the bag down as he checked his pocket watch nervously.

'You say that he's been there all night, Iron Eyes?'

The bounty hunter nodded. 'Yep!'

'Strange,' the marshal muttered.

Joshua screwed up his face in a pained expression. 'Maybe he's going visiting someone.'

Iron Eyes rested a hand on the wooden porch upright and glared at the man who suddenly looked excited. The tall, thin bounty hunter tilted his head as a stagecoach came along the street towards the depot.

'Joe Brewster was staying in the hotel,' Iron Eyes said as he watched the stage come to a dusty stop opposite them. 'He had himself a couple of heavy bags when he arrived. Bags full of golden eagles! Anyone find that loot?'

'Nope!' Joshua answered. 'Come to think of it, nobody seems to have set eyes on any of that gold coin since that outlaw got his head blown off.'

'We found two empty bank bags in

Kelly's office but only a few coins,' the marshal added, then looked across at the hotel manager again. This time with knowing eyes.

'C'mon!' Iron Eyes nodded. He stepped down into the street and began to walk towards the stagecoach and the man who had intended being its passenger.

Bale and Joshua trailed the tall bounty hunter to the tailgate of the stagecoach as its driver vainly tried to lift Carter's hefty bag and stow it at the back of the vehicle. Iron Eyes raised a hand and silently stopped the driver.

'Leave the bag, driver.'

The driver obeyed and backed away.

Rufe Carter stepped to the edge of the boardwalk. 'What's the meaning of this?'

The lawmen paused on either side of the bounty hunter.

'Who is this, Marshal?' Carter asked, looking at the tall man clad in Cyril Perkins's best funeral clothing.

'This is Iron Eyes, Rufe,' Bale replied

looking at the swollen bag before returning his attention to the small, neatly attired man. 'You going someplace?'

Carter nodded. 'To my sister for a little vacation.'

'This your bag?' Iron Eyes asked in a hushed tone.

'It is.' Carter looked afraid.

'Mighty heavy by the looks of it,' Joshua noted. 'What you got in there?'

Carter knew the game was up. He sat down on the edge of the boardwalk, cradled his head in his hands and then began to sob like a child. 'I knew I'd never get away with it. But I had to try. Damn it all, I had to try!'

Iron Eyes reached down to his boot and pulled out the long-bladed Bowie knife. The morning sun danced along its lethal length as the hotel manager briefly looked up. Carter screamed. The men watched as the hotel manager fell back in a faint.

'Kinda emotional, ain't he?' The deputy shrugged. 'Anybody would think that he thought Iron Eyes was gonna stab him or something!'

The bounty hunter sliced through the leather straps on the top of the bag and revealed the glittering fortune in golden coins inside it. He picked up one of the coins and bit it. He smiled, then slid the coin into his pocket. 'You can have the rest of them.'

'There might be a reward for finding this money, Iron Eyes,' the marshal said. 'Could be a tidy sum!'

'I've got more than enough bounty coming.' The bounty hunter sighed and rubbed his throat. 'Damn, I'm thirsty.'

'How'd old Rufe get his hands on all this money, Monte?' the deputy asked as he stooped over and gazed into the bag.

'Maybe Rufe stole it when Brewster left it in his hotel room,' the marshal suggested. 'He has a master key which'll open every damn door in the hotel. Maybe the temptation was just too great for a man who never had nothing better than a nagging wife.'

'Well, glory be!' Joshua grinned. 'Who'd have thought Rufe was that smart? You gotta hand it to him. They do say it's always the quiet ones you have to watch out for. Cunning little devil, ain't he?'

Iron Eyes dropped the knife back into the neck of his boot, turned and began to walk away.

Bale raised a hand to his mouth and called out, 'Where you going, Iron Eyes? You ain't bin paid the reward money yet and the bank won't be open for another hour.'

The bounty hunter paused for a moment. Then, without looking back or answering, continued on walking towards the nearest of the street's many saloons. It was also where he had earlier tethered his magnificent palomino stallion. The marshal and his deputy watched as the man dressed in the secondhand funeral clothes entered the Silver Bell.

'You know something? Iron Eyes still makes me a tad nervous, Monte,'

214

Joshua admitted.

Bale clipped the back of Joshua's head.

'Ouch! What was that for, Monte?'

'I'll think of something,' Bale replied.

We do hope that you have enjoyed reading this large print book.

Did you know that all of our titles are available for purchase?

We publish a wide range of high quality large print books including:
Romances, Mysteries, Classics
General Fiction
Non Fiction and Westerns

Special interest titles available in large print are:
The Little Oxford Dictionary
Music Book, Song Book
Hymn Book, Service Book

Also available from us courtesy of Oxford University Press:
Young Readers' Dictionary
(large print edition)
Young Readers' Thesaurus
(large print edition)

For further information or a free brochure, please contact us at:
Ulverscroft Large Print Books Ltd.,
The Green, Bradgate Road, Anstey,
Leicester, LE7 7FU, England.
Tel: (00 44) **0116 236 4325**
Fax: (00 44) **0116 234 0205**